HENDRIX

GUARDIAN GROUP SECURITY TEAM BOOK 2

BREE LIVINGSTON

Edited by
CHRISTINA SCHRUNK

Hendrix: Guardian Group Security Team Book 2

Edited by Christina Schrunk

https://www.facebook.com/christinaschrunk.editor

Proofread by Krista R. Burdine

https://www.facebook.com/iamgrammaresque

Cover design by Book Covers for $20

http://www.facebook.com/stunningcovers

Bree Livingston

https://www.breelivingston.com

Publisher's Note: This is a work of fiction. Names, characters, places, and incidents are a product of the author's imagination. Locales and public names are sometimes used for atmospheric purposes. Any resemblance to actual people, living or dead, or to businesses, companies, events, institutions, or locales is completely coincidental.

Hendrix: Guardian Group Security Team Book 2 / Bree Livingston. -- 1st ed.

ISBN: 9798729469376

To Christina,

Here's to the last three years of being my editor. You're still the best. Thank you for making my books read-able. You've pushed me to be a better writer, and for that, I am eternally grateful.

1

A *text?* Really? On a Friday night?

Britney Wolf stared at her phone screen, mouth agape and gobsmacked that her date had just dumped her—using a text message of all things. Some of her friends were recipients of that type of rudeness, but up until a second ago, Britney could say she'd never had that happen before.

Trent was supposed to be picking her up in fifteen minutes. If she'd known he was going to break the date, she wouldn't have wasted time getting ready. And she'd so looked forward to it. He was a little shorter than she liked, but he was cute, sweet, and she loved his humor and wit. Dates with him were fun because they ran in the same circles, giving them a little more in common than the last two guys she'd dated. This was supposed to be their fifth date, too. Perhaps it was just as well as there was really no spark between them.

Another text from Trent popped up. *I'm sorry, but I just can't handle the weird threats. I got two today. One this morning at work, and one just now.*

The next text was a picture of a pink stuffed pig with its head ripped off and a written note warning Trent to stay away from Britney.

Groaning, Britney pouted. "Not again." It had been a couple of weeks since she'd received anything. She thought for sure they'd stopped, not because it was about Trent, but because she thought they'd moved on.

I like you, Britney, but this is just creepy. It's just...I don't want to be dealing with this. This probably makes me look like the bad guy, but this has been going on since we started seeing each other a month ago. You're cute, but...well, I'm sorry. Hope you find someone who can deal with it.

For the last six months, she'd been receiving stuffed animals and flowers from someone anonymous. At first, she thought it was cute because the idea of a secret admirer was sweet and a little fairy-tale-ish. She suspected it was someone who needed time to work up the courage to talk to her and she needed to be patient.

She'd never received anything even remotely threatening, but the few men she'd dated had—and it was a stuffed pig with its head ripped off. As soon as she stopped seeing someone, the person would stop. It sent the first guy running after the very first pig. The second lasted a little longer, but he'd eventually put on his running shoes too. She couldn't blame them, but it was just a pig. No warnings. No gory stuff. Just a stuffed animal. So benign she'd thought it was a prank at the beginning.

Kicking off her heels, Britney slogged to the bed and sat, her shoulders sagging as she mourned the loss of yet another potential relationship.

Whoever it was, the person sending her little gifts needed to either step up or step away. At least that's what she'd thought before they'd started with the threats. Surely they knew her well enough to know she wouldn't laugh in their face or something else equally rude. They had to know she'd never treated anyone as though she were better than them.

A knock came from her door, and Britney lifted her head. "Come on in, Mom." Now that her brothers were married, it was just the two of them. Twenty-nine and still living at home. Most her age would consider that a failure, but Britney loved her mom.

"I just got home," her mother said as she pushed the door open and then stopped short. "Another one?"

Pushing off the bed, Britney nodded. "Trent broke our date." This was the third man the secret admirer had chased off, and she'd yet to tell her friends and family about it. No one had been hurt, and she didn't feel the need to worry the people she loved, especially when the person was most likely harmless.

If Noah knew, he'd have organized an all-out war. Being the owner of a private security company and ex-military, her brother took any and all types of perceived threats seriously. Which was wonderful for his clients, but it made him extra protective. Sweet, but Britney didn't need a SWAT team.

Yes, this person sent things to her dates, but who could take a decapitated stuffed animal seriously? If it was that easy to run them off, then it was likely that they'd ditch her the second life got hard. Britney wanted a relationship like her mom and dad. He'd passed away a few years ago after battling a brain tumor. It had changed his personality, making him a horrible person, and her mom had stuck with him. Britney wanted the kind of love that was action, not all talk.

Her mom crossed the room and enveloped her in a hug. "I'm sorry, sweetheart. You'll find your someone soon. I know you will." The scent of hay and horse clung to her mom's clothing.

Britney wrinkled her nose. Normally, she loved the smell, but it seemed like she'd rolled in something other than just hay. "What on earth happened at the boarding facility?" she asked, leaning back.

Dropping her arms from Britney, her mom huffed. "You know that little pony I told you about? The one who thinks he owns the whole place?"

"Yeah."

"Well, he decided he didn't like how I smelled today, and as I was brushing down Jasmine, the turkey knocked me down. Needless to say, the floor wasn't particularly clean."

Covering her mouth with her hands, Britney tried to hold back laughter. "Oh, Momma."

"Guess it's a good thing I have that old pickup. I'll have to have the stench cleaned out, but at least it's not the Jeep." She shook her head. "I ordered pizza on the way home, and if you keep laughing, I'll make you eat a green pepper."

Snickering, Britney walked to her dresser. "Fine. You go take a shower while I get comfortable. I think this night calls for a movie and some serious chocolate gluttony." At least she was heading for Hawaii on Sunday for her friend Ruby's wedding. She was ready for a relaxing break on the beach.

Her mom walked to the door. "The pizza should be here in about fifteen minutes. I'm going to take a shower, and then we can eat."

"Okay, Momma."

"All right. I'll see you downstairs." Her mom quietly shut the door behind her.

Britney strolled to the bathroom to slip out of her "wow 'em" dress and into her fat pants. Once her hair was pulled up and her contacts were out, she left the room and walked downstairs.

The house felt so empty as of late. Of course, her siblings *did* visit. Most often it was her brother, Zach, and his wife, Harley, along with their daughter, Kenna. Britney loved that they lived not too far away. She didn't begrudge her brothers and sister for having families; she just wanted one of her own.

Reaching the first floor, she walked to the living room and grabbed the remote. It had been a while since she'd had a night with just her mom, and she had to admit, she enjoyed those nights. If there was one thing her dad's passing taught her, it was that she needed to treasure people while she had them.

The chime of the doorbell sounded, and she walked to it, pulling it open. Smiling, she said, "Hi."

The delivery guy pulled the pizza out of the warmer bag, and the smell was divine. "Here ya go."

For a second, she could swear she knew him. Something about his eyes looked familiar. There was no name tag to help her place him either. He'd probably just delivered their pizza before. "Do I owe you?" Britney asked.

"Nope, paid online." He smiled. "Thanks for ordering Pop's Pizza Pies. Have a good night."

Britney waved and shut the door with her foot. Peeking inside, she grinned. Her momma had not decided to torture her with green peppers. Instead, it was their shared favorite: mushrooms, tomatoes, and onion, with circles of melted mozzarella on each slice. Her mouth watered as she crossed the room and set it on the coffee table.

"Well, that's good timing." Her mom walked into the room with her hair in a turban. "I'm hungry, too." Just then, the doorbell rang, and she said, "Are you expecting anything?"

Shaking her head, Britney began flipping channels. "Nope."

Her mom held up her hand. "Oh, you know what, I bet it's for me. I ordered a new medicine organizer. The one I have is about to fall apart."

A loud gasp from the doorway caught Britney's attention, and she crossed the room, stopping next to her mom. She wilted. A stuffed unicorn that looked like the one from *Despicable Me* was perched on the door-mat. So far, her admirer had left things when no one else was home. That's how she'd kept it hidden for so long. Why had they changed delivery methods this time?

Britney peeked outside the door. It didn't make sense. How was anyone able to put something on her porch and get away so quickly? It wasn't like they had a ton of places to hide, either. She glanced skyward, wondering if maybe a drone had been used. Nothing. So odd.

"What is this?" Britney's mom looked at her.

"Everyone knows I love *Despicable Me*. I bet it's just one of my friends."

Her mom stooped down and picked it up, snatching a small note before it drifted to the floor. "Britney, what is this?" She held the note up where Britney could read it. "This looks like a threat."

Taking the unicorn from her mom, she tucked it under her arm. "It's nothing. Probably just a prank."

"Britney. That does not sound like a prank." Her mom's tone had that I'm-not-playing-with-you-kid sound to it. "It says, 'I'm watching you.'"

"It's really nothing, Mom." Britney turned and walked to the couch, tucking her feet under her as she took a seat.

Her mom followed her. "Nothing?" She set her hands on her hips. "You tell me right this instant what's going on."

Groaning, Britney lifted her gaze to her mom. "I didn't say anything because it's harmless, and it's nothing."

"Say anything about what? What's harmless?" Her mom stared at her, her gaze growing intense.

"For about six months now, I've had a secret admirer. They've sent me little stuffed animals about once a week. Up until two weeks ago, when they stopped. This is the first one I've received since then."

Her mom's mouth dropped open. "Are you telling me you've had a stalker and said not a word? Britney, what were you thinking?"

"Mom, it's harmless. All they've done is send stuffed animals. Granted, the few guys I've dated would say it's —" She clamped her lips together and squeezed her eyes shut.

"The guys? Wait, are you saying Michael, Ray, and Trent received this stuff as well?"

Britney's shoulders sagged. "Yes, they have, but as soon as they stop seeing me, their gifts stop." At least, that's what Michael and Ray had told her, and she had no reason to believe Trent would be any different. Although, she'd never expected to receive something when her mom was home either. Hopefully, Trent would let her know if his gifts continued.

"What kind of gifts were they getting?" her mom asked, taking a seat next to her.

"Stuffed pink pigs with their heads torn off."

"Britney Lee Wolf, you're just now telling me? How long were you going to keep it hidden? Did you at least let Noah know?" The words rushed out, and Britney could see fear in her mom's eyes.

Shaking her head, she said, "No, I haven't told him either. This is the first time I've gotten a note. I went out with Trent a little longer than Michael or Ray. I guess the person was upset."

Her mom palmed her forehead. "Oh my stars in the heavens. Do you have any idea how dangerous it was not to tell us?"

"Momma, it's probably just someone afraid of talking to me. They're just working up their courage. Once that happens, everything will be fine. If they were dangerous, they would have done something by now."

"Britney, baby, I love how kind your heart is. You're patient and loving, and I admire that most about you, but this is serious. We *have* to call Noah."

Britney's head dropped back. "No, Mom, he's going to flip out, and our house will be Fort Knox in less than twenty-four hours."

Taking Britney's hand, her mom gripped it tight. "And with good reason. You're going to Ruby Garcia's wedding in Oahu in a couple of days. What if this person follows you? This isn't something to trifle with."

Britney hung her head. "Momma."

"Either you call him or I will," she said, letting go of Britney's hand and squaring her shoulders. "I don't care how harmless it feels. It's not. And you should have never kept it from us."

"This is why I didn't want to tell anyone. It's making a mountain out of a molehill. There's no reason to call him."

"And you aren't upset nearly as much as you should be. Noah needs to know."

This was not an argument Britney was winning. Well, at least she didn't have to hide anything from her mom anymore. Maybe it was better this way. Noah would figure out who it was, and the person would be forced to confront her. Then the whole thing would be done and she could get on with her life.

2

Getting a call from Noah, his boss, just before dark wasn't typical, but Hendrix Wells didn't mind. Usually in situations such as this, it was an urgent case, and whoever was requesting help was in immediate danger. Most of the time, clients were met at the Guardian Group headquarters and the case was discussed in the office or conference room.

Guardian Group Security provided help to people who'd exhausted all other options and didn't have the finances for their own protection. One of the many reasons Hendrix loved working for them. Rich or poor, Guardian Group helped people, which made it easy for someone with his past to pay penance.

The group had been started years ago by Pamela Williams after her husband was murdered and she found he'd left her a substantial fortune. She'd given the reins to Noah when she found love again, and he'd been running it since.

With his luggage in one hand, Hendrix climbed the steps of the airplane and stopped just inside. "I'm here and ready to go."

Noah looked up from where he was sitting and waved him over. "Thanks for getting here so quickly. I know I told you it was personal. Are you sure you're okay working on it?"

Hendrix nodded as he walked to the seat across from Noah and sat. If Mia and the kids were in trouble, someone would pay. "I'm fine. Okay, what's going on?"

Noah paused for a moment as the door shut and the engines fired up. "My mom called a little bit ago, and someone is stalking my baby sister, Britney."

Okay, so Hendrix's circle of protection was expanding. Noah was a good man, a great boss, and held a loyalty Hendrix didn't afford to too many people. Hendrix's upbringing didn't leave room for spreading trust around with careless abandon like most. Although, since joining Guardian Group, the number of folks he was willing to take a bullet for, aside from clients, was growing. That list now included Britney Wolf, but only because of her connection to Noah.

Noah shuffled a few pictures lying on the table

between them. “They’ve been sending her little presents the last six months. Today, she got one with a note telling her she’s being watched. According to my mom, the three men she’s dated since it started have received warnings with stuffed pink pigs with their heads ripped off.” He swore under his breath. “And this is the first I’m hearing of it.”

Six months. Little gifts. All the men were getting them too. Hendrix ticked off the details, committing them to memory. “Why did she keep it from you?”

“Other than my wife and Mom, Britney is...well, special. She’s patient to a fault, has never met a stranger, and the only enemies she has—which are very few—have hurt people she loves. She is loyal, intelligent, and kind. Sometimes a little flighty, but it’s more of a lovable quirk. It doesn’t matter what you look like, how you dress, or what your bank account holds, she treats everyone equally.” Noah heaved a heavy sigh. “And she insists that there is good in everyone. Even when that might not be the case.”

Hendrix envied his boss, talking about his family the way he was. Hendrix and his brother, Walker, had been separated roughly nineteen years ago when Hendrix was 11. They’d only recently reconnected, and their relationship was tenuous at best. The one fact they agreed on was that the rest of their clan wasn’t worth knowing. Truth be told, Hendrix lumped himself in with the rest of his emotionally bankrupt family. Mentally, he quickly fortified his well-built wall. Memories were great for other people. People who had worth.

"What's the plan, then? Does she have any idea who it could be?" Hendrix asked.

Noah shook his head. "I don't know. My mom called, near-hysterical, and told me I needed to get to Houston because Britney was in trouble. I told her I'd be there in a few hours. I dropped everything, gave Ryder the helm, and came here."

Again, envy bubbled in Hendrix. Well, it wasn't just Noah. Ryder and Kennedy heightened his envy too, maybe even more so since they had Rufus. That dog was less animal and more human. He'd come to the rescue a few times. His name was first on Hendrix's take-a-bullet list.

When Hendrix was first recruited, he'd struggled with the dynamics of the place. Everyone seemed like family, which for a regular person would have been great, but not him. Those folks were the first to stab you in the back. Actually, trusting anyone was a risk as far as he was concerned.

"Hopefully, Britney will give us enough that we have something to work with. If not, it's going to be a needle in a haystack. Plus, she's got a high school friend's Hawaiian wedding to attend this weekend."

"Then she can't go. Not if we can't find the threat in time."

Blinking, Noah chuckled. "Yeah, um, I'm going to let that go. You wouldn't believe me anyway, so it's just best to experience Britney in person."

One eyebrow crept upward as Hendrix grinned. "Are you *scared* of your sister?"

Noah snorted. "No, she's just..." He stopped and seemed to be searching for words. "Seriously, just wait until you meet her."

Did Hendrix want to meet this woman? She certainly intrigued him, and he didn't often find himself in that type of situation. *Off limits,* his head screamed while his heart did backup vocals. Not only was Britney a client now, but she was his boss's little sister. She was the human equivalent of the red button of no touching.

If either of those two reasons didn't send a strong enough warning, there was also the matter of Hendrix's past. He slammed the brakes on his errant thoughts. There was no need to entertain them.

During the flight, Noah discussed a few hypothetical possibilities and what they could do to find the person responsible. That's if she had any idea of what precipitated the first gift. A party, a date, or whatnot. As a very wealthy Houston socialite, there were any number of ways she could have found herself an obsessive fan.

A few hours later, they were pulling into the circular drive of a two-story brick home that *Better Homes and Garden* would feature, or Hendrix expected as much. Little lights pointed at the flower beds set against the base of the home, giving him a tiny grasp of the grandeur. In the daylight, he suspected it would be even more so.

Noah parked and cut the engine in the front of the home. Before he reached the top step, an older woman opened the door, meeting him midway and embracing him.

"Hey, Mom," he said. They hugged a few moments. "It's not like you didn't see me last month." He laughed.

"And that's a month too long to go without seeing my baby." She looked at Hendrix. "Come on in."

As Hendrix passed through the entryway, he took note of the light feel of the house. It wasn't dark and stodgy like most homes of the well-to-do. This felt more like a family lived in it. He looked at the wall just inside the entry filled with pictures of a happy family.

How different things might have been had he experienced what Noah had. A lifetime of love and support as opposed to a couple of years. In that respect, he suspected he was lucky. Most folks like him didn't get a second chance, but he had in the form of a cop who'd seen potential in a kid going nowhere.

"Hendrix, this is my mom, April," Noah said. "Mom, Hendrix Wells."

Turning, Hendrix smiled and shook the woman's hand. "Nice to meet you."

"Oh, posh," she said, yanking on his hand and pulling him into a hug. "This is Texas, sweetheart, and I'm a hugger. Thank you for helping us."

He smiled as she hugged him and replied, "My pleasure."

"We had pizza, so Britney's changing shirts." April smiled.

"She sauced herself?" Noah asked, laughing.

"First slice."

Noah looked at Hendrix. "Running joke. Britney can't eat pizza without somehow getting it on herself."

April hooked her arm in Hendrix's. "Now, I know it's nearing midnight, but could I offer you something to drink, to eat?"

"Uh, actually, I'd love some sweet tea if you have it."

She looked at him, mocking offense. "If I have it? You mean some people don't have it? What a sin." She winked.

Hendrix grinned. "I didn't grow up in the South. I'm

from the central part of the country. I got hooked on it when I joined the Marines."

"A Marine?" She leaned back, and her eyes sparkled. "My great-granddaddy was a Marine." The two of them crossed the expansive living room to the kitchen, and she pointed to a spot at the island. "Let me get you that tea."

A distinct squeal that usually came at seeing a family member filtered in from the room they'd just left. Britney must have found Noah. He was good people. If anyone deserved a loving family, it was him.

"You have a nice home, Mrs. Wolf," Hendrix said.

"You call me April. Mrs. Wolf makes me sound old. Do I look old to you?" She gave him a pointed look, daring him to say otherwise.

He laughed. "No, ma'am. Not a day over twenty-five."

April smiled. "My son always hires the smartest people."

Voices grew louder, and a moment later, Noah stepped through the entryway. A woman pulled up next to him, and Hendrix's world tilted. Britney Wolf.

His friends had often described the first time they met their significant other like it was a magical moment. Time slowed, and the details of the woman they'd eventually fallen in love with were highlighted in such a way that they never forgot it. Hendrix had thought it was ridiculous, a story to tickle the ears of their significant other. But he couldn't have been more wrong.

As if what he was experiencing needed confirmation, her electric-blue eyes locked with his, and his breath caught. Of course, appearance-wise, she was beautiful. That was a fact, not a feeling.

Guessing from the bulk of the dark hair haphazardly pulled up into a bun, he'd bet it cascaded past her shoulders, easily. Apple cheeks, pink Cupid's-bow lips, and a heart-shaped face rounded out the angel standing in front of him, looking at him expectantly. That aside, something about her gave him the sinking feeling that his soul was on a collision course with hers. A feeling that equally terrified and excited him.

"Uh, Hendrix?" Noah's voice pierced through his stupor.

"Yeah, sorry." Hendrix didn't get tongue-tied. He didn't get wrapped up in a woman. With his past, there was no reason to. And yet, he could picture himself with Britney in his arms, content to let the world burn. "Hi," he said, sticking his hand out to shake hers.

The very second her hand slipped into his, it was all he could do not to yelp and flinch away. Had he known he'd get electrocuted, he'd have worn better-soled sneakers.

"Hi, I'm Britney. It's nice to meet you," she said with

a voice as sweet as her appearance with just a hint of Southern drawl. "Thank you for indulging my mom and brother."

He needed to snap out of it. This was his boss's little sister. Emphasis on the whole sentence. She was out of his league. Completely, wholly, and totally. "No problem."

She gripped his hand, turning the underside of his forearm up. "Oh, that's pretty." She stepped closer, lazily tracing the cross tattoo that ran the length of it. His breath caught as the friction of her fingers against his skin left invisible scorch marks. She lifted her gaze to his again. "I bet there's a story to go with that, isn't there?"

Yep. One he'd never shared but found himself desperately wanting to tell her. Mentally, he punched himself in the face. His jets didn't need to cool; they needed manual override and then to be disassembled. Boss. Sister. Client. He introduced his ducks to the row he was forming.

"There is, but it's boring." He smiled, working to keep the tingles skirting over his skin from showing on his face.

Her eyes twinkled. "I doubt that."

Noah cleared his throat. "Let's hear about that stalker." His gaze drifted from his sister to Hendrix.

Britney dropped her hand from Hendrix's arm and

walked to the stool next to Noah to sit. "Fine." She rolled her eyes.

Hendrix's heart skipped a beat and pounded once like a gavel and then skipped twice more. Never was there a time he could recall a woman affecting him in such a way. Noah had said his sister was special, but even with the warning, Hendrix felt ambushed.

If one look caused him this much internal havoc, this case needed to be solved and quickly. He needed to be on the quickest possible ride out of Houston. His heart had dealt with as much heartache as it could handle. He had a feeling if Britney got ahold of it, he'd never find all the pieces. He'd risk his life, no problem. His heart? Not a chance.

3

Britney swam to the edge of the pool, braced her hands on the tile surround, and hoisted herself onto the edge. "Noah, I've given you all I remember." At least twice since the night before, and he was still having her *start from the beginning*.

"And no one stands out?" The question came out like he couldn't believe she had no idea.

Shaking her head, she said, "No. If they did, I'd tell you."

Noah grumbled. "All right. I just wish you'd told me sooner."

"I know, and I'm sorry. Hand on a Bible, Noah, I really didn't think it was a big deal." She twisted to look at him. "Yesterday was the first time I got a note."

Standing, Noah wiped his brow with the back of his hand. "I'm going inside to give this list of locations you've visited over the last couple of months to Ryder, and I'll be right back. Hopefully, he's able to pull camera feed from something and gives us a clue."

"Okay." Her shoulders sagged. "I'm sorry, Noah. I wasn't trying to be difficult or put anyone out or—"

"It's okay, sis." He smiled. "I'll be back in a minute."

Once Noah was out of earshot, Britney looked at Hendrix. "I'm sorry to you too. I've made your job harder."

Not nearly as sorry as she should have been. What a hunk and a half of a man. Tall, dark hair, dark eyes, and olive skin. His shirt stretched across what she suspected was a toned chest and stomach and seemed to hide plenty more tattoos beyond what she could see on his arms.

The same tingles she'd experienced the night before came rushing back as the scene played in her mind. Tracing his tattoo, the goosebumps that had broken out. The way her pulse had gone from zero to sixty in a millisecond. It was a novel feeling when it came to her physical reaction to a man.

"You might have made my job a little hard, but we'll find 'em. We always do." Hendrix chuckled. "Don't worry about it." His gaze stayed pinned on the ground at his feet like he was avoiding looking at her.

The light blush covering his cheeks made the reaction cute and endearing. Most of the men who ran in her circles didn't seem to care if they stared. It added to his attractiveness.

"Easier said than done." Two steps, and she was sitting in the same chair Noah had occupied. "You know you could go swimming."

Shaking his head, Hendrix said, "No, I'm okay." Again, he avoided looking directly at her, still just as cute.

She balanced her elbow on her knee and put her face in her hand. The impression she got from him was that he didn't like bringing attention to himself, either because of choices he'd made or the way people had treated him in the past. One of the things she took pride in was reserving judgment of books until she'd read the first chapter or two. In his case, she suspected he was a bestseller. "I know what you're thinking."

"I doubt that." He shot her the sexiest lopsided smile to ever grace a man's face. "Everyone I've ever met has been fresh out of pennies, and I wouldn't take the offer if they did."

Narrowing her eyes, she straightened. "If I guess

correctly, will you go swimming?" She flicked her gaze heavenward, stood, and sat on the wicker sofa beside him. "Better angle."

Wow, those eyes of his.

She'd noticed them right away, but this close, staring into them was a treat. One light brown and the other deep blue, and equally soulful. "Heterochromia."

He blinked and jerked his gaze away. "Uh, yeah."

"Don't ever pull away because of that. You have beautiful eyes. A woman can have the best of both worlds when she looks at you."

When he returned his gaze, their eyes locked. "Um."

Tilting her head, she could picture herself with his head in her lap, staring into those dual-colored eyes for hours. He was a book she wanted to dive deep into. Discover the mysteries that made him who he was and celebrate the choices—whatever they might be—that ultimately led him to sit across from her. Maybe getting Noah involved wasn't so bad.

She shook her head, stilling the thoughts. They'd just met. What if he had a girlfriend? "So, we got a deal?"

A few heartbeats thumped by. "Sure." Skepticism coated the word.

Just as she opened her mouth, a faint buzzing sound

caught her attention. She squinted and pointed. "*What is that*?"

Off in the distance, a tiny black speck grew closer until she could see that it was a drone carrying a package. As she went to reach for it, he stepped in front of her. "Don't touch it. We don't know what it is."

In one swift move, Hendrix grabbed the towel she'd planned to use to dry herself. He waited a breath and then flung it out like a blanket in the hopes of covering the drone. It quickly zipped to the side and dropped the package before zooming away.

"What just happened?" Noah asked as he rushed out of the house and to the package on the ground. "The security cameras went wonky for a second."

Hendrix tipped his head toward the sky. "A drone. It dropped that package. We haven't touched it."

"Good. I've got some friends close by who can check it out for us."

"It just flew into the backyard and then flew away." Britney was dazed. Nothing like that had happened before. "Just flew away."

Turning to Britney, Hendrix took her by the arms. "You okay?"

She looked at him. "Yeah, I'm fine, just taken off guard. What if I'd been by myself?"

"But you weren't. I won't let anything happen to you.

You have my promise on that." He put his arm around her shoulders. "I think we should go inside just in case the operator has any more ideas."

"Yeah, I need to make a call," Noah said.

A few hours later, the owner of a chemical detection company was waving goodbye after giving the all-clear on the delivery. The drone signal was found, and Guardian Group had notified local police. They'd found it in a dumpster roughly a mile away, but with that range, there was no way to tell where it had come from.

Outside by the pool once more, April hugged Britney around the shoulders as Noah and Hendrix opened the box. "Honey, please be careful," her mom said.

Noah glanced at her. "I am."

With the tape cut, he pulled the flaps of the box open and took out the contents. "A stuffed heart?"

"And a note," Hendrix said, picking it up and opening it. "'I said I'm watching you. That means I know where you are, who you're with, and everything else.'"

A chill like cubes of ice slid down Britney's back. "That's creepy."

Hendrix looked at Noah. "There's no way we can let her go to a wedding in Hawaii."

Britney scoffed, cocking her hip and lifting a single eyebrow. This man needed an education on Texas women. "Oh, yes I am. I'm in the wedding. I'm not canceling because someone is trying to wreck my life." Plus, she'd made a promise to her friend. One she wasn't going to break.

Shaking his head, Noah set his hands on his hips. "I'm with him. There is no way I'm letting you go to Hawaii when you're being threatened."

She pulled away from her mom, holding her finger up. "I *am* going."

"Britney, this person is threatening you. How am I supposed to protect you if you're in Hawaii?" Noah stepped closer. "You can't go."

Grumbling, she pinched her lips together. She was going to that wedding, but how? Her mom and Noah would team up and strap her down if she didn't figure something out.

Her gaze drifted to Hendrix, and she grinned. Now that Trent had dumped her, she was minus her plus-one. "I have an idea."

Noah shared a look with Hendrix. "Okay," Noah replied. "Let's have it."

"First," she said, directing the question to Hendrix. "Are you single?"

"Uh...yeah." He drew the last word out like he was trying to find the rest of the sentence.

"Let's draw this son-of-a-gun out. He doesn't like me

dating, so how about I pretend to date Hendrix?" Britney smiled sweetly. "So far, this person only seems to get cranky when I'm seeing someone. Who better than a big ole strong hulking fella like him?"

Hendrix's eyes widened. "Date? As in…you and me?" His finger wiggled between them.

"It's perfect. We're staying at a resort with our own private little huts. Ruby's uncle just finished it. They're using the guests as guinea pigs so they can write it off on their taxes. I'll get our room numbers." She looked at Noah. "You can have guys go ahead of us and set it up. Hendrix can keep watch while I'm there." She shrugged. "If this person is that obsessed with me, there's no way he won't follow."

Noah scratched his chin.

"We really should stay put. We've got a solid security system put in, and we can get the house covered by team members who switch off." Hendrix set his hands on his hips. "Whoever it is will eventually slip up, and we'll catch them."

Britney's eyebrows went to her hairline. "So…you want me and my mom to be prisoners in our home? I won't do that to her."

"Honey, if it'll help catch the person, I don't mind," her mom said.

Turning to her, Britney softened. "That's not fair."

"Actually, the fake-dating thing isn't a half-bad idea," Noah said. "We could be here for who knows how long before we caught the guy. If we goad him into action, it might trip him up." Noah looked at Hendrix. "Britney, let me talk to him for a second."

Britney looked from Hendrix to Noah and nodded. "Sure, Momma and I will see what we can scrounge up for lunch."

As she turned, she cut a glance at Hendrix. The poor thing looked petrified, but she'd make sure he knew she didn't bite.

The moment they were inside the house, her mom waggled her finger at Britney. "That fella was about to come unglued, and you know it."

"I need a plus-one anyway. I was going to ask Trent, but he dumped me." She glanced over to the door. "And Hendrix is just so cute."

Her mom's mouth dropped open. "You like him."

Britney waved her off. "I just met him, but I'm serious about the stalker. This person has been doing this for months, and it's been the same thing the whole time. Something needs to trigger him to come out of his hiding place."

"I guess, but Hendrix was sheet-white."

He was, but Britney had the feeling he needed a friend. She'd been a friend to a lot of people. When it came to secrets, she was the person everyone turned to. She liked having that honor. And something about Hendrix tugged at her gut-deep. Whether anything more than friendship would ever come out of it, she wasn't sure. But friendship? She was certain about that.

4

Hours later, Hendrix was still flummoxed by his encounter with Britney. Wolf certainly suited her; that was for sure. She gave the appearance of a sweet, innocent woman, but in reality, she was dangerous. He had no doubt she could take a man's heart and bite a chunk out of it, and the fella would walk away thanking her. Not that she did it in a malicious way, just a natural side effect of her alluring personality.

"Just try it on." Britney held the shirt up to him again. "It brings out your eyes."

He looked down at himself, perplexed with his current situation. "I'd look ridiculous in this."

Britney's plan was awful, and yet, there he was, standing in the middle of a clothing store with her, picking out clothes for a week-long stay in Hawaii. As her boyfriend. He wasn't even sure how it happened. His brain had formed a hard *no.* He'd been all set to flat-out refuse, and the next minute, his tongue had gone rogue and he'd accepted the assignment.

The one thing he couldn't deny was the attraction. In all his years on earth, he'd never met a woman who'd set a hook in him so hard and fast as she had. It didn't matter that she was his boss's little sister. Something about her bright, infectious personality called to his soul. But she didn't know him. If she did, he had no doubt she'd be like all the rest. Running away as hard and as fast as they could.

"This place is too expensive. You really shouldn't spend this kind of money..." he said, leaning in, "on me." The store had shirts with three digits before the ninety-nine.

She curled her hands in, pressing the shirt to her chest. "You didn't bring clothes for a trip to Hawaii, and I saw the look on your face when I suggested my plan. The least I can do is make this a little more comfortable while we're there. You'll need more than what you brought because Ruby has special things planned." She caught his gaze and stepped closer. "And what if I think you're worth every penny, maybe more?"

His breath caught. That was a new one. Someone

thinking he had value? He lowered his gaze to the floor. "I'm not."

She used her finger to tip his chin up until her eyes were locked with his. "*Yes*, you are."

His heart bolted out of the gate at the shot of her touch. It was creating havoc on his nerves. He kept his eyes locked with hers. "You get your way a lot, don't you?"

"Maybe sixty-forty."

He chuckled. "More like a fraction less than a hundred."

She playfully smacked his arm and pointed to a rack near the wall of dressing rooms. "Get to picking."

"Fine." He groaned and walked to the display of swim shorts. He had no intention of swimming. He hoped that the stalker would make a move quickly and this case would be over. The less time he spent with Britney, the safer he'd be.

Skimming through the trunks, he glanced at her. Man, she was beautiful. She'd worn white ankle-length pants with a yellow off-the-shoulder top. With her dark wavy hair and sun-kissed skin, she was a sight to behold. The whole outfit appeared to be an outward extension of her bubbly, bright personality.

She walked from table to table, touching the fabric of different shirts, wrinkling her nose here and there.

One out of four would seem satisfactory, and she'd set it over her arm. Even more interesting, she was picking shirts with colors and styles he liked, which meant she'd been observant. Most women would have picked out what they liked, but not her.

He needed to not think about it too hard. This would be over in a flash, and he'd be back in North Carolina on another assignment.

"I found you a suit," she said as she stopped behind him.

He turned, a grimace on his face. "A suit?"

She rolled her eyes. "It's a wedding. Of course there's a suit involved." Handing him the pieces she'd gathered, she tipped her head toward the closest fitting room. "See if this stuff fits?" It came out more like a question than a demand. Another trait he found attractive. "If it does, we can call this shopping trip done and over."

"Sure," he replied as he took the second load of clothes from her.

He walked to the fitting room where they'd been setting the stuff he liked while they browsed. In the room, he paused as he looked at the clothes she'd just handed him. All the shirts were made of a soft material, some even softer than the stuff he'd chosen earlier. It was sweet and thoughtful.

"Would you mind letting me see the suit when you

try it on?" she called from just outside the dressing room.

"Sure." It would be the last thing, though. Suits made him feel stiff and weird. His childhood hadn't required any suits. Mostly, he was thankful when he had something that wasn't filled with holes and didn't reek of cigarette smoke.

After trying on a few of the shirts to see how they fit, he picked out several he liked and set the others aside. Then he did the same for the jeans, shorts, and trunks he'd picked out.

"Everything okay in there?" Britney asked.

"I guess. The shirts are fine, and the shorts and jeans are good." If it were anyone other than her, he might be offended by the jeans. He'd brought plenty of those, but they weren't designer. She'd meant what she said about making sure he didn't feel out of place.

He picked up the dark blue suit and looked it over. He wasn't so sure about this choice. "Are you serious about this suit?" he asked as he began putting it on.

"With the ivory dress shirt, please. Give me any lip, and I'll make you wear a tie." The tiny laugh gave him a vision of her with a twinkle in her eye and a smile on her face.

"You'd have to wrestle me to the ground for that to happen." He laughed, returning the tease.

"Who says I wouldn't do that anyway just to see if I could," she shot back.

Everything stilled except his pulse, and his thoughts skidded to a stop. For a moment, he wasn't sure how to reply. He stuck his head out of the dressing room and found her sitting in one of the plush armchairs. "I was joking." Mostly.

Holding his gaze, she rolled in her lips, trying to keep a straight face. "I wasn't."

This woman. Hendrix slowly exited the room, smiling as he pointed his finger at her. "That's not funny."

"Be still my heart, Mr. Wells." She stood and walked closer, tilting her head one way and then the other. "That looks really good on you."

They were not seeing the same dude in the mirror. "I can't pull this off."

She closed the little bit of distance left, swept his hands away from fidgeting with the collar, and straightened his shirt. "You sure can." A flirty smile played on her lips.

All he could think was that he didn't want to disappoint her. "I just don't want to ruin your trip. I think one of the other guys—"

Her fingers touched his lips. "I'd rather have it

ruined with you there or not take anyone at all." She dropped her hand.

"But I'm...I'm broken. I don't..." If she only knew how ugly his past was. Why was he even saying anything? He needed to draw a line so he didn't end up hurting her. He shook his head and pulled himself up to his full height. "I'll be fine. I appreciate you taking the time to help me blend in with the rest of the people who will be there."

Nodding, she stepped back, narrowing her eyes at him. "I don't know what just happened, but I won't push. When the storm clears, I'll be standing right here." Her smile returned, and she patted his chest then sashayed back to her chair.

Britney Wolf was a force of nature bottled and shaken up like soda, with Mentos thrown in. Instead of destruction left in her wake, the need to be near her, soaking up her sunlight, propelled him to follow her in the groove she left. Never had he wanted to be in a woman's orbit more than he wanted to be in Britney's. If all he got was a lingering warmth, it would be worth it.

With the clothes he liked picked out and the dark blue suit that seemed to make her happy, they left the store and drove a few blocks to a ratty-looking burger joint.

"This place is ugly as sin on the outside, but the food

is sinfully good." She paused while he grabbed the restaurant door. Catching his gaze, her lips quirked up. "I've found that I like the inside of beat-up things. They tend to be worth more."

His tongue retreated to the back of his throat while his heart pounded in his chest. Every time she looked him in the eyes, it felt like she was peering into his soul. "Not all the time."

"Eye of the beholder, Mr. Wells, eye of the beholder." She patted his chest and sauntered inside.

Closing his eyes, he worked to put himself together. If this was what he had to look forward to for the rest of this trip, he was going to come away more bloodied and bruised than ever. He had to put a stop to all this flirting. His heart couldn't take it.

Maybe he needed to gently extricate himself from this situation. He respected Noah and would do anything for him, but his sister... Noah could have better prepared him for Armageddon. This woman was a world shaker in kitten heels.

With himself stitched together a little better, he followed Britney inside. A small wait later, and the hostess took them to a booth and left them with menus. They sat in tolerable silence until Britney lowered her menu just enough that he could see those piercing cornflower-blue eyes.

"If you aren't comfortable going to Hawaii with me, it's okay to back out. I'd never make someone do anything they didn't want to." She lowered the menu a little more. "It won't hurt my feelings. Maybe my pride because I'll be down a plus-one."

The courage he'd mustered just moments earlier bucked at his determination to step away. "It's too easy in situations like these to send mixed messages and blur lines. Too easy to forget that it's not real." He caught her gaze. "I'm not someone you want in your life. You need to know where I stand so there's no miscommunication." He breathed a silent sigh of relief that he'd managed to get that all out and sound convincing.

Her gaze lowered to the table. "I'm a big girl, Hendrix. My big girl pants are all the way to my chin, and I'm more than capable of looking after my heart." She lifted her gaze to him again, a smile on her lips. "However, if you think this could pose a problem to... one of us, I'll gladly tell my brother to find someone else."

"I hate to say it, but I think it might be a good idea. I'm just not the right guy for this, and you need to be kept safe. I'd hate for something to happen because feelings were hurt."

Shrugging, she looked down at her menu. "Okay, we'll eat, and I'll return the clothes. I'm sure whoever

Noah picks will be fine. If they're willing. Either way, I'm going to that wedding."

Inwardly, he groaned. The very second Noah considered Britney's fake-boyfriend idea, Hendrix should have counter-argued or refused to participate with the latter being the best option. Clearly, where Britney was concerned, his decision-making skills were questionable. He'd already hurt her, and they'd only gone shopping. His head and his heart could argue all they wanted. He'd made the right call.

5

Her big girl undies could be pulled so high she had a wedgie, and Britney would still be disappointed. For whatever reason she couldn't put a finger on, she liked Hendrix, and she'd looked forward to spending some time with him. Sure, he was different than the guys she'd been interested in before him, but she felt at ease with him.

At this point, she didn't want Noah to find someone else. She was drawn to Hendrix. She didn't know if it was his smile or the way he looked at her, or the whole package. She just knew someone else would be a huge let-down. Going to Hawaii alone was better than dragging someone else along, and with the way she'd responded to Hendrix in the store—him or no one—

going alone was exactly what she'd be doing. *Not* her finest moment.

A waiter stopped at their table. "I'm Chris. I'll be your waiter this evening." He clasped his hands in front of him.

She stared at him a moment. "Do I know you?" she asked. Much like the pizza guy, his face seemed incredibly familiar, but she had no idea where to place him. His name didn't ring a bell either.

"I don't think so. Unless you come here a lot." His voice didn't ring a bell either.

"Okay, I guess you have one of those faces." She stopped trying to search her memory and sighed. "Sorry."

"It's okay." He shrugged.

With their drink orders placed, Hendrix leaned forward. "*Do* you know him?"

"For a second there, I thought so, but no, I don't. The name isn't familiar either." She picked up her menu, studying it again. "I was probably just reaching for a culprit."

"I'll try to get a picture and send it to Ryder. Maybe he can do his magic and figure out if he's been at any of the same functions." Hendrix leaned back. "I doubt it takes us too long to catch the person. Dating that Trent guy seemed to trigger something. Perhaps there was more there than you think. If the stalker wasn't in the picture, would you still be seeing him?"

The question was simple enough, but neither *yes* nor *no* seemed to be the best answer. Would the relationship have continued? She hadn't thought about it in those terms. "Maybe. I don't know. All my friends are getting married..." That could be part of it too. Seeing people finding their soul mates and settling down. How was it so easy for them and so hard for her?

"They're getting married, and I wonder what could be wrong with me that no one wants me." She inhaled a deep breath before letting it out slowly as her mouth launched into autopilot mode. "I hid the stalker from my family, which was stupid and incredibly reckless, but I think there was a small part of me that liked being desired and wanted. Not that I don't think I'm loved, but a soul mate isn't the same as a family member or friend."

Shaking her head, she dropped her hands to her lap and closed her eyes. "I'm sorry. That was a long-winded answer."

Movement jerked her attention to Hendrix, and the next thing she knew, he was sitting next to her. He stretched his arm across the back of the booth as he leaned in. "There's nothing wrong with you. Somewhere out there, a guy is waiting for you. He's wishing and hoping and praying that he'll be lucky enough to find you and all the wonderful things you have to offer. He'll never be worthy, and he'll know it. But he'll step over mountains to try if it means he gets to spend the rest of his life with you."

She blinked back tears. "Thank you. That was very sweet." She forced as much vibrancy as she could into her voice.

He tilted his head, his eyes boring into hers. "I meant every word I said."

"I know." She patted his leg. "I'm fine."

"Britney, this is why I don't want to go through with your plan. I don't want to hurt you." His intense gaze held hers.

"I know, and you haven't. You asked me a question, and I answered. I may have overshared, but I'm fine. Right as rain."

Hendrix took his arm from the back of the seat as he nodded. "Okay, just wanted to make sure." He stood and took his seat across the table from her again, picking up the menu. "So, what do you suggest at this place?"

"I'm not the best person to ask. I like just about everything." She set her menu down and folded her arms in her lap. "I'm going with the Lucy in the Sky with Habanero."

"'With a hint of Reaper'?" The pitch in his voice rose with each word. "You know those things are beyond hot, right?"

"I can stand a lot more heat than people give me credit for. I'm not fragile, Mr. Wells."

Hendrix dropped his menu on the table. "I feel like I've upset you and you won't admit it."

"I'm not upset at all." With his line of work, perhaps he was used to the damsel in distress. "I'm fine. If you want something with less heat, I'd try one of the burgers with or without jalapeños."

"All right."

The waiter returned with their drinks and left with their entrée order. Awkward silence fell between them and stretched to an almost painful length. If they were going to Hawaii together, she'd be asking him questions, trying to get to know him. Part of her still wanted to do that, but she refrained.

Instead, she pulled out her phone and texted Noah, starting with her plan not happening.

What? The return text was almost immediate.

Noah, I'm a lot of things, but I'm not going to force him into attending a wedding with me. He seems incredibly uncomfortable, and I don't want to spend a week in paradise with someone who doesn't want to be there. It wouldn't work anyway. Dating is hard enough. Pretending is worse.

Let me talk to him.

No, she quickly tapped out. *We're at dinner. I was just texting you so you know. If there happens to be someone else willing to go, maybe you can find them between now and the time we get home. I'm leaving tomorrow morning.*

If I can't find someone, that means you can't go.

She worked her jaw, flicking her gaze to Hendrix who seemed engrossed with his own text conversation, and returned her attention to her phone screen. *We'll discuss it when I get home.*

No discussion. No date, no go.

Do you want me to call Mia? It was a last resort, but one Britney knew would work. Minutes ticked by until finally another text popped up.

We'll discuss it when you get home.

Britney grinned like she'd won a prize. She put her phone away and went back to twiddling her thumbs. When she'd suggested they have dinner after they finished shopping, she'd had an entirely different scene in her head.

She touched her tongue to her teeth, thinking about what Hendrix had said earlier. He didn't want to hurt her. Why did he think he held such power? A burning question she now felt compelled to ask. "May I ask a question?"

He looked up from his phone. "Sure."

"What makes you so adamant that you'll hurt me?"

His color didn't just drain; it whooshed away like it was snatched off his face by the Reaper himself. "I...I'm not. I'm just saying I'm not the guy."

"Why? You protect women all the time, don't you?" She held his gaze.

"Well, yeah, but I don't fake date them." He set his phone facedown on the table. "I just make sure they're safe."

For a moment, she ruminated on the answer. "Is fake dating that out of the ordinary? Aren't there times that call for out-of-the-box thinking?"

"Sure there are." Color was returning to his face, and his body language screamed frustration.

She took a deep breath, nodding. "Okay, then I have to ask, do you have some sway over women that would put me in such danger that you can't perform your job?"

The slight catch in his breath made her work to keep her face straight. She'd hit a nerve and hit it hard. He wasn't used to women who pushed back against his defense. "No, I can do my job just fine. I just don't think I'm the right guy for *this* job."

"Then that begs the question, are you afraid of me?"

She touched her chest and smiled, batting her lashes and using the sweetest voice she could muster.

"Uh, no, I mean, no. It's just..." A needle on a scratched record didn't stammer as much as he was. "I'm not afraid of you."

"I see." She sat back, holding in a gut-bust laugh. "So, you don't have an animal magnetism so great as to wield power over women. You've thought outside of the box before, and according to you, you've done a fine job. And, I'm not the reason you can't do your job this time. So, then...what am I missing?"

His head dropped to his chest with a groan.

She touched her fingers to her lips to help her hold in a snicker as she watched him. It was hysterical that he could be so easily flustered. "No worries," she said, cutting her line so the fish could go his merry way. "I was simply curious."

Lifting his head, he leveled his gaze at her. "I was wrong. You get your way one hundred percent of the time."

"Well, now, if that were true, I wouldn't be going to Hawaii without you now, would I?" She grinned.

Slowly, a smile stretched on his lips. "You're infuriating, you know that?"

Man, he was fun. "It may have been mentioned in

the past by one of my siblings, but I chalked it up to bias and not an actual accusation."

The waiter returned with their orders and set their plates in front of them, along with a bottle of ketchup to go with their fries.

"I can smell that wicked sandwich all the way over here," Hendrix said, picking up a fry and using it to point to her plate. "That has stomachache written all over it."

"Maybe for *some* people." She laughed.

Pinching his lips together, he shook his head, muttering something under his breath she couldn't quite make out. "You...are trouble."

She made a sound like she was wounded. "Oh, this little exchange makes you think I'm trouble. Perhaps you aren't the man for the job after all."

He lowered his gaze, shaking his head. "Just...just eat your burger."

"Yes, sir."

His head hung lower as he grumbled a little more.

Oh, he plum tickled her. He was too cute when he was flustered, and she liked the way his eyes twinkled when she teased him.

She was right. The women he'd met were easy to push away. They took all his barking as an indication he'd bite, but she had a feeling what he'd wanted was someone willing enough to brave the fear and scratch him behind the ears.

Too bad she'd let him out of the trip. It would have been a delight to get to know him. She had a feeling he was something special. Someone who'd been hurt and still forged ahead.

Once they were finished eating, they left the restaurant and went to the car. A small distance from the car, she pressed her key fob, and Hendrix put his arm out, stopping her.

"Wha—" The question died on her tongue as she spotted the note hanging from the driver's side mirror. "'I'm watching you,'" she read, her voice wavering. "Why me?"

Hendrix pulled her into a tight embrace. "I'm glad you invited me to Hawaii. I can't think of a better way to spend my week."

She leaned back, her eyebrows drawn together.

As if sensing her question, he smiled. "Thank you for thinking of me and including me in your plans."

Well, she loved that, but knowing he hadn't wanted to go, she palmed his chest. "It's okay if you can't."

"Nope," he said, pressing his lips to her forehead. "It's a great way to spend time with my girl."

Ohhhh...the light bulb clicked on. She knew what he was doing. If the stalker was watching, he was getting an eyeful. It was smart thinking on Hendrix's part. Still, his lips had touched her skin, and her nerves buzzed with energy. It didn't take much to realize Hendrix had been right. If she wasn't careful, he could hurt her without even trying.

6

The very second Noah spoke Britney's name, Hendrix should have walked off the plane. The woman was...frustrating, irritating, aggravating...brilliant, observant, witty, and charming. Just when he thought he was free, he was swallowing another worm.

Currently cruising at thirty thousand feet, she was sitting across from him, gazing out the window of the private plane she'd secured.

He'd been all set. She'd offered him an out, and he'd taken it. For sure, he was in the clear, and then she'd started with her questions. He was a moth to a flame. No, the moth at least had a good reason for getting itself burned. What was his? She'd literally asked if she could ask a question, and like an idiot, he'd said *yes*.

In less than five minutes, she had him so tongue-tied he didn't know which way was up. There was nothing sixty-forty about the woman. That smile of hers, the way her cheeks rose as her lips lifted. The sparkle in her eye, or better, the mischief. She knew it, too.

When he'd asked about Trent, she'd sat back, a thoughtful expression on her face. Then she'd poured her heart out. For her to even speak the words that something might be wrong with her had floored him. Wrong with her? Okay, maybe she could have been a little less intense, but he had to admit he kinda liked her putting a hook in his mouth.

"Thank you," she said softly.

"For what?" he asked.

She set her head on the back of the seat and rolled it, looking at him. "For being my plus-one. You didn't have to, and you did. I just want you to know I appreciate it."

"You're welcome." She didn't need to say it, but the fact that she did spoke to her character.

To him, there hadn't been a choice. He'd seen the note, and his heart had stopped, so he'd done the most logical thing. Okay, maybe logical was the wrong word. She was in danger, and he'd promised he wouldn't let anything happen to her. He'd covered himself by hugging her and saying he looked forward to the trip in case the stalker was nearby, and then he'd kissed her on the forehead. It was a natural reaction that a man would have taken and a huge mistake. It had taken four glasses of tea to cool his lips off.

The annoying question niggling in the back of his mind was why he'd changed his decision. Was it him or her? The answer wasn't nearly as easy as it should've been.

They'd waited at the restaurant for Noah to arrive. On his way to them, he'd spoken to the police, and they'd taken photos at the scene. The street cams were useless. Ryder found nothing on those.

Lifting her head, Britney smiled. "So, tell me about yourself."

"Uh, I'm from Arkansas." True, but he was leaving out details. She didn't need those to fake a relationship with him.

"Any siblings?"

"One. His name is Walker. He's got a year left on his contract with the Marines. He may come work at Guardian, but we'll see." That's if he wanted anything to do with Hendrix. There was a chance their relationship was better at a distance. "If I recall correctly, you have four."

"I do." Their eyes locked a moment. This was the part where parents were usually discussed, and he was bracing for it. She took a little breath. "So, how did we meet?"

It was like she knew, but that wasn't possible. He'd honed his craft of not showing his cards. He didn't have a tell, or so he thought. Maybe she just didn't want to know. That was probably closer to the truth. "We could just say we met through your brother. It's the truth and one less lie we have to keep up."

"Good idea. Did we just strike up a conversation and find each other palatable? Or was there electricity and fireworks and world-tilting?" She grinned.

"That sounds like a part of the backstory you'd tell better." Because for him, it was the latter. He was still crispy around the edges, and that was before he'd known how soft her skin was. Or how well she fit against him. How much he liked holding her. Kissing her...

This trip had plenty of glitter and zero gold.

A little after two, they arrived in Oahu and took a rental car to the resort. Hendrix wanted to have a vehicle in case anything came up.

"I sure love this island." Britney's voice was bright.

"I've never been to this one, but I've been to the Big Island. It was beautiful." He glanced at her. "How many times have you been here?"

She cleared her throat. "Quite a bit, actually, especially in the last few years with my friends..." The sentence trailed off as her voice grew soft. Not a second later, her smile was back in place. "But it's always fun." She sat forward. "Oh, hey, we're here. Wow, Ruby's uncle did a good job. Look at all those flowers."

Lush was a good word for the vegetation that greeted guests. He turned off the road, expecting to see the lobby, and found it set back at least a half-mile from the road, making it feel like he was entering another world.

When he reached the overhang, Britney opened her door and stepped out. "I'll go check us in."

"All right." His excuse for watching her go was that he needed to keep an eye on her. Not that he enjoyed it.

Guardian Group had spoken with the resort management, and without divulging names, they'd upgraded Hendrix and Britney from single-person rooms to a bungalow. It allowed for all the monitoring equipment and kept Hendrix close in case the stalker tried to hurt her.

Hendrix hated it but couldn't deny the logic. A week in Hawaii with Britney was going to be hard enough as it was, and now he'd be sharing the same space. It was like the universe was testing him, adding layer upon layer of hurdles he had to jump.

A car pulled up beside him, and a single guy got out. Hendrix set his thoughts aside and watched the man. As Britney met him on the way out, they stopped, and

Britney threw her arms around him. Hendrix's heart was a bucket filling with jealousy as the man swung her around and then set her feet back on the floor. These thoughts needed to quit. She could hug and swing around with anyone she wanted.

She laughed and nodded, and if Hendrix had to guess, she'd just made plans to talk to him later, no doubt catching up on whatever part of their lives they'd missed.

"Who was that?" Hendrix asked.

"Just a guy I went to high school with. David Goss. I didn't even know he'd be here. His dad has a real estate firm in Morocco, and he just returned to the States about six months ago after working there. He's here for the wedding too." She looked in the direction of the lobby. "He's sweet. We bonded over dissecting frogs in Biology. Both of us thought it was disgusting."

Hendrix leaned forward, his eyebrows knitting together. "Do you think he could be the stalker? Timing fits."

"David? No," she said, returning her gaze to Hendrix. "He's never been interested in me like that. We've always just been friends. It was nice seeing him, though."

"How do you know he was never interested in you like that?" Hendrix was on alert. It seemed convenient that this guy would show up just as the stalker began sending her gifts.

Shrugging, she replied, "Well, probably because he dated a lot of girls in high school. I don't think he dated anyone for very long. A few months at best. Not a womanizer. His parents had a terrible divorce, worse than my mom and dad, and I think he was scared of that happening to him."

"Or maybe the girl he was really interested in didn't appear to have a mutual attraction, so he used them as surrogates." Hendrix gave her a hard look. "It's happened before."

"I'm sure it has, but that's not the case for me and David."

Hendrix eyed the lobby once more and then put the car in drive. "Okay." He'd be giving that guy's name to Ryder, just to be thorough. If he happened to have a skeleton, it was only right to find it and give the information to Britney.

They reached the bungalow, and Hendrix parked the car in the attached carport. He'd been to plenty of nice places, but this one outshined them all. Private and peaceful. Not only did he get to hang out in Hawaii, but he got to stay in a great room with a great girl.

A girl who was not his and would not be his. All he

could do was pray that whoever was looking down on him would please let him find the stalker quickly.

Britney stepped out of the car and pointed her nose to the sky, taking a deep breath. "I love that salty smell and the crash of the waves."

"I can't disagree," he said, popping the trunk of the car as he stepped out.

She walked to the back of the car to get her bag, and as soon as he realized what she was doing, he picked up his pace. "I can get that."

"It's okay. I'm more than capable."

"I didn't say you weren't. I don't mind doing it."

Her smile lifted a little more. "All right. Let's go check out this bungalow."

Grabbing the rest of the luggage, he followed her to the small courtyard outfitted with a table and four chairs. She used the keycard, pushed the door open, and held the screen door so he could pass by.

"This kind of has a wow factor, doesn't it?" Hendrix asked.

The rooms were separated by an open-area living room, kitchen, and attached dining space. Light, bright, and modest. It was luxurious without feeling pretentious. From the door, he could see sliding glass doors covered with a sheer curtain that allowed him to make out the ocean not far beyond.

She stepped in behind him. "Yeah, it does. Makes you want to take up permanent residence."

"Sure does." He set his luggage down and took hers to her room.

Since Guardian Group didn't want anyone wondering why all the equipment was in Hendrix's room, they'd covered his window to keep out prying eyes.

When he returned to the small living room, he found Britney at the back of the bungalow, looking out the sliding glass doors as she held the curtain aside. She turned, letting it float back in front of the glass doors. "I think I'm going to get on my suit and go sit outside a while."

"Just let me get my stuff put up, and I'll go with you." He was supposed to be protecting her, his head reasoned. His heart merely gave a frustrated groan while forcing a vision to flicker in front of his eyes. One of him holding her as they enjoyed the beach.

"I'll be all right."

"No. I need to go with you."

"You can't tell me my brother doesn't have a camera pointed out that way. You'll be able to keep watch over me from your room. If there's another drone, I'll just scamper inside." She crossed the area and stopped at her bedroom. "No need to worry at all."

Even knowing she was right, it still didn't feel like a good idea to let her go by herself. If that David fella decided to pay a visit, Hendrix needed to be there...as her boyfriend. Because that was his job.

He searched for a reason to stick close. "We need to make this believable. Sell it. If we're a couple, it stands to reason we'd go out there together."

"Or you have a headache, and being the sweet boyfriend that you are, you didn't want to keep me from enjoying myself." She grinned.

It was as if she had an answer for every reason he had for going. Like...like she didn't want him anymore. But he didn't want her to want him, right? Shaking his head, he tried to chase the thought away. He'd have a nervous breakdown before this trip was over if he didn't get himself together. "That's a good reason. I'll get things set up, then."

"Good. I'll see you later." She walked into her room and shut the door.

Snatching his luggage handle, he stomped into his room and texted Ryder that they'd arrived safely and Hendrix would do a check on the equipment to make sure it hadn't been tampered with. Dwelling on things wasn't going to put his mind at ease, but maybe a little distraction would help.

Hendrix walked to the wall of monitors and turned

it on. In a blink, video feed from cameras placed all over the resort was coming in clear. Including the one Britney guessed about.

A moment later, he heard her door open, and then she came into view sporting a large sunhat and a one-piece suit with a sarong tied around her waist. Even in black and white, she looked good.

He grumbled. So much for a distraction. Now he wanted to see how much better she looked in color. He was never, never taking a case like this again. For once, his heart agreed. Because he was positive there would never be another woman with the pull Britney Wolf had.

7

With each deep breath, Britney said a silent thank you to Ruby for having her wedding at her uncle's new resort. She'd needed this little getaway. It was pure pleasure letting the mixture of sea, salt, and sand clean her lungs as the light breeze kept it from being too warm. The little umbrella anchored in the ground was a nice touch too.

"A quarter for your thoughts."

Shielding her eyes from the sun with her hand, she leaned forward a little and grinned at David. "I don't have twenty-four pennies to give in change."

He laughed and shook his head. "Mind if I join you?"

She gestured with her hand. "Join away."

"I'm kinda grateful to Ruby for letting me come

early." He plunked himself next to her about a foot away. "I needed the break from real estate."

"I didn't realize people could come early. That's nice. Has work been rough?"

Shrugging, he drew up his knees and laid his arms atop them. "A little. Part of the reason I returned to the States was how burnt-out I felt. I thought the change in scenery and maybe being back among friends would help, but I seem to be working just as hard here as I was there."

"Sounds like you need balance."

"I do." He looked at her. "How about you? I saw Zach a couple of weeks ago. He said you were helping his wife with planning events." He shook his head. "Which I have to admit, when he said wife, I wondered if I was losing my hearing. He was never getting married."

Britney belly-laughed. "Did he tell you how he met her?"

"I was rushing to meet a client, so he didn't get the chance."

"He was flying medical equipment to Jamaica, and a storm forced a crash landing. By the time they were rescued, he was head over heels. Honestly, it's rather romantic if you ask me. I love Harley. She's perfect for him."

Something Britney wanted. Not perfection, just

perfect for her. For a split second, she wondered about Hendrix. It was an odd feeling for a man she'd known for such a short time.

David scooted closer. "There's that thinking face again."

She blinked and brought her focus back to David. "I'm sorry. Just tired from traveling." That was partly true. There were errant thoughts about why she was still without someone special.

Touching her shoulder, David caught her gaze. "I'm here if you need to talk."

"Thanks," she replied, covering his hand with hers. "I appreciate the offer." Something held her back from really considering his shoulder to cry on, so to speak. She pulled her hand back at the same time he did.

"Hey, I couldn't find my swim trunks at first," Hendrix said as he came into view, his gaze darting from Britney to David.

There was no comparing the two men. David was clean-cut, no tattoos, moderately built. Attractive with his dark eyes, dirty-blond hair, and flashy smile. Just her cup of tea. Normally.

Then there was Hendrix. He was a couple of espressos knocked back and a shot of pure caffeine in a Formula Five Hundred Solo cup. He'd worn a shirt with his swim trunks, but it was cut off at the shoulders, displaying his toned arms, which she'd suspected. Not vein-popping, but there was no question he worked out.

Then there were the tattoos littering both arms. On his left, a date and long piece of script wrapped around his upper arm like a tribal band. On his right, an American flag with a soldier kneeling and a few more random ones that seemed disjointed, like he'd been lost for a while.

She'd almost asked about his parents on the plane, but she'd caught the slight variation in his voice, and she was sure he didn't realize he'd shifted a few too many times. If he wanted to tell, he would. She wasn't going to press the issue.

"Uh, David, this is my boyfriend, Hendrix." She smiled. "Hendrix, this is David. We went to high school together."

David pushed to his feet and shook Hendrix's hand. "Nice to meet you, Hendrix."

"It's nice to meet you too." His voice held an edge as he looked at her. "Ready for a swim?"

"Actually, I think—" She directed the words to David.

"It's okay. I don't want to interrupt." David took a step back. "I'll see you later."

"Sure." She smiled.

As soon as he was out of earshot, she looked at Hendrix. “What was that?”

“What was what?” Hendrix’s eyebrows knitted together, almost making him look angry. “We’re supposed to be dating. Are you telling me the guys you’ve dated would have been okay with some guy they don’t know just showing up and sitting down next to you? Placing his hand on your shoulder?”

She stood to face him and tilted her head. “Probably.” The answer shocked her, but it was true. They wouldn’t have cared because they knew as well as she did that their relationships weren’t going anywhere. “They weren’t serious about me, and the feeling was mutual. And David is a friend from high school with zero spark.”

The anger seemed to melt away. “Then they weren’t good enough for you to start with.”

She grinned, shrugged one shoulder, and started for the water. “True.”

“Wait,” he said, grabbing her arm. “I was serious when I said we could go swimming.”

“Are you sure? I don’t want you thinking you need to do anything you don’t want to.” That was the honest truth. If he went places with her, she wanted him to want to go. Dragging him by the collar would only wear her out.

His lips pressed together as he stared at her. Then his posture softened. "I appreciate that, but it's not a chore to spend time with you. You just...fluster me."

"Me? I'm harmless." She chuckled.

"If by harmless you mean you're a Venus flytrap, then sure."

Why did that admission tickle her so? Perhaps to someone else it was an insult, but to her, it was him admitting he was attracted to her, even if he didn't want to be. Oh, the fun she was going to have.

She leaned back a little, batting her lashes, and mocked shock. Then she lifted an eyebrow. "Does that mean you're a helpless fly?"

Balling his fists, he swore under his breath, but she could see he was trying not to smile. "Do you want to swim or not?"

"Are you sure you want to frolic with someone as deadly as me?"

Then he did something she would never have seen coming. He tugged her to him, wrapped those behemoth guns he called arms around her, and buried his face in her neck. "You..." He sighed. "I'll think I'll take my chances."

It was for show, but that didn't mean she couldn't enjoy it. She slid her hands up his muscled chest and hooked her fingers behind his neck. "Care to share your odds at surviving?"

The grin he shot her made her glad he was holding her up. Fake or not, that smile was a woman-wrecker. "Most likely, horrible."

She pulled free and smacked him on the stomach, just before taking off for the water. About waist deep, he grabbed her from behind and lifted her out of the water. She swatted at his hands. "You better stop it!"

"Hey, this isn't a fair fight. I have to act when I can."

A second later, water covered her head and rushed up her nose. Her feet found the sand, and she straightened, pushing her hair from her face as she surfaced the water and wiped her eyes. Oh, she was about to murder someone. He was bigger than her, though, and revenge was a dish best served cold. "All right. I would have dunked myself sooner or later."

His eyes narrowed. "Why does that scare me?"

"I'm not even half your size." She folded her arms over her chest. "Why you'd be scared of little ole me, well, I just don't know."

"One hundred percent." He closed some of the distance and mirrored her. "You don't even know what sixty-forty looks like."

She rolled her lips in and raked her gaze from the

top of his head to his watery toes. "I didn't get my way in this one. You volunteered."

"After you came up with the plan." He dropped his arms to his sides. "And it wasn't like I had a choice."

"No choice? You most certainly did." She wrinkled her nose. "Admit it. You like me." Whew, this was fun. He was fun. She sure liked him, and it didn't matter if it was mutual.

He opened his mouth like he was about to speak but stopped and worked his jaw. Looking away, he shook his head and then returned his gaze to hers. "I don't know how anyone could ever *not* like you."

She closed the rest of the distance, palming his chest. "Well, I do like you. You're fun to tease."

In one swift movement, he picked her up by the waist and held her in the air a second. She for sure thought he was going to pitch her like a log, but at the last second, he pulled her to him. "I don't mind being teased by you."

Everywhere his skin touched hers, she was on fire. Not only was he deliciously gorgeous, but he was also funny and sweet. And she'd never felt safer in a man's arms. But this was also fake, and they were in public. Anyone on the shore, including her stalker, could see them. That was the only reason he was holding her like he was.

"Okay, I think I've had all the sun I need for right now. I'm going to go inside, take a long bath, and get in a small nap before dinner tonight." She stepped back. "You gonna stay?"

"For a second." He smiled. "Have a good nap."

"Thanks." After she splashed her way to shore, she passed by the umbrella and snagged her sarong and hat. As she got to the bungalow, she paused and watched him a second. He'd dunked himself and was raking his hands through his hair.

Oh, my, my. Yeah, this trip was going to be interesting for sure. There was also a chance he'd been right. Her heart was about to get a beating if she wasn't careful.

8

"I'm ready when you are," Hendrix called from the living room. The new clothing had him feeling out of place. Slacks? Dress shirt? Yes, he'd worn nice clothes before, but they hadn't felt like this. Then again, he hadn't wanted to impress anyone before, and no matter how many times he tried to deny the feeling, it didn't stick. He wanted Britney's approval.

The door opened, and she stepped out. "I'm ready." She ran her fingers through her hair and lifted her gaze to his, smiling. "I knew that would look good on you."

He'd dressed casually because that's what he was told to wear, but she was anything but. Her dark wavy tresses fell below her shoulders with a shine that gave it a silky appearance. He immediately devised a plan that would allow him to run his fingers through it. Just to make sure he was right about its softness. Adding to the wow factor was a flowy one-shoulder dress that matched her eyes and glittery silver heels that showed her painted pink toenails. Better yet, she was the perfect height for kissing. An activity he didn't need to be thinking about.

It had taken several dunks in the ocean to get his skin cooled off enough that he could walk to the bungalow. Then he'd taken a cold shower. She was so cute. He loved sparring with her.

He'd made the worst mistake when he'd pulled her close. It didn't matter how much clothing he wore, his skin was electrified when it was touching hers. If she hadn't stepped back when she had, he would have no doubt kissed her.

"Wow. You're...you're..." He was grasping for words that, even if spoken, wouldn't do her justice. "Stunning." And he wanted to take her in his arms, blow off dinner, and kiss her until he had his fill. He pushed the thoughts away. They'd be late if he had to take another cold shower, and he'd have to have a good reason to shower again, which he didn't have.

Her lips quirked into a sexy smile, and her eyes twinkled as the light from the evening sun poured through the back door. "Thank you."

He held his arm out. "I'm hungry. How about you?"

She slipped her arm through his, and he no longer had to wonder what it was like to have the most gorgeous woman in the room standing next to him. It didn't matter which room or who attended, Britney took that title effortlessly.

Just before they stepped out, Hendrix set the alarm and shut the locked door behind them. They'd gone a few steps before she took a deep breath, leaning against him.

"You know you came to my rescue by coming with me." She squeezed his arm.

"I'm certain I should be the one thanking you. It's not often a man gets to say he's with the most beautiful woman in the world." He shot her a smile.

She laughed. "Just you wait. Those guys are only going to be jealous 'cause their girls are looking at you."

His neck grew warm, and the heat spread to his cheeks and blistered a trail to his ears. He'd been told he was attractive, and it had washed over like nothing. Apparently, the person giving the compliment was what made him blush. Which was correct, and he was certain the title would belong to Britney for the rest of his life.

The remainder of the walk was spent in silence. Each time he tried to untangle his tongue enough to speak, a new battle would break out between his head and his heart. He felt like a bystander, watching the two forces pitted against one another. How could he pick the winner when he didn't think he'd be able to declare one?

At the door to the restaurant, a man in a tuxedo welcomed them and waved them through. Hendrix wasn't sure what they were having, but he knew he'd be hurting when they left. Whatever it was, it smelled amazing.

Inside, a hostess verified they were on the guest list, grabbed two menus, and led them to a large banquet area. Several couples were already seated, some sharing the larger tables. Hendrix felt he'd lucked out in that they had a table to themselves.

They'd just taken their seats when a woman with flaming red hair stopped at the table. Britney stood, embracing her. "Hey, Ruby. You look gorgeous tonight. Just as gorgeous as your inside. Doug is a lucky, lucky man, my friend."

Ruby's face took on the color of soft rose. "Thanks. What do you think of the resort?" Her bright red lipstick stood out against her pale skin. Freckles filled her forehead and splashed across her nose. She was pretty...and Hendrix was sure her fiancé was lucky.

Britney bounced as she laced her fingers together in

front of her. “It’s amazing. Thank you for treating me—us—to something so wonderful.” She turned to Hendrix. “This is my boyfriend, Hendrix Wells.”

Ruby shook his hand as he stood. “It’s nice to meet you. I’m glad you could come.” She turned back to Britney. “If you need anything, let me know. I’ve got the schedule of events being emailed to everyone tonight during dinner. I would have had it out sooner, but we had to switch one of the events. We’re snorkeling instead of visiting the cultural center. You’re going to love it. It’ll be so much fun. And I look forward to seeing how you two do in the Couple’s Quiz.” The woman waved bye and strolled to the next table where a couple had just been seated.

Hendrix groaned. “Couple’s Quiz? That should be fun.”

They took their seats again, and Britney laid open her menu. “Don’t worry. You don’t have to go if you’d rather not. I’m just glad we get to order what we want tonight. Catered events are nice, but sometimes I really don’t want chicken or beef. Sometimes, I just want a salad and a dessert.”

As Hendrix flipped open his menu, a live band began playing music. He’d missed it when they first walked in because the carpet blended with the stage. He couldn't help but wonder how many had tripped over that thing.

Britney smiled, and Hendrix twisted in his seat to follow her line of sight to the entrance. David. That guy again. Of course, Hendrix knew the man would show up because Ruby knew him well enough that he could arrive early. That didn't mean Hendrix had to like it.

David followed his hostess to a table where five others were seated. Instead of immediately taking his seat, he crossed the room and stopped about a foot from Britney. "Hey, did you have a good swim earlier?"

"I did," Britney said, angling herself toward David. "Did you get to go swimming?"

He slipped his hands into his pockets, shaking his head. "No, unfortunately, I had to work."

"Well, that stinks. You need to say no next time. You can tell them you're visiting with an old friend you haven't seen in ages." She smiled.

Hendrix worked to keep his face and tone neutral. "The water was great. You definitely need to take a second and enjoy it."

David turned to him. "Easier said than done sometimes. This fire was put out, though, so I should have the remainder of my time free."

Maybe it was the inflection in David's tone or the slight

bulge in the neck vein, but Hendrix got the sense he was being put on notice. This guy was declaring war and making a play for Britney. Fake boyfriend or not, David was going to end up with a fist in the face if he tried anything. There was a plan, and he and Britney needed to stick to it. It was the best way to catch the stalker, even if this was the first time Hendrix was agreeing with her about that.

Hendrix met David's unspoken challenge head-on. "Good. I made sure my calendar was free before I got here. Boundaries, you know."

As David went to speak, a waiter broke the spar by greeting them. David touched Britney's shoulder and winked. "I'll talk to you later."

"Sure," Britney said before David walked back to his table. Her eyebrows knitted together as she looked at the waiter. "Do I know you?" She narrowed in on his name tag. "Greg. I feel like I do."

Hendrix eyed the guy. Same height as the waiter at the restaurant in Houston, but this guy had red hair. If it was a dye job, it was a really good one because it didn't seem fake. He pulled out his phone, keeping it hidden by the table, and shot a text to Ryder. As soon as he got a photo, he'd send that too.

The man shook his head, smiling. "I don't think so."

"Okay," she said, but it looked to Hendrix like she was searching her memory.

With their drink orders made, the waiter left them. "Do you know him?" Hendrix asked.

Shrugging, she cast her gaze to the table. "For a second, I thought he kind of looked like the pizza delivery guy on Friday and that waiter last night, but his teeth are wrong. The other guy didn't have a gap, and this guy did."

"Wait. The pizza guy?" Hendrix asked.

"Yeah, he didn't have a nametag. His eyes seemed familiar, but there wasn't anything extra distinguishable about him. I didn't really pay attention too hard. I'm sure he'd just delivered our food before. Mom and I do order pizza a lot."

Hendrix nodded and pulled out his phone. "I'm texting Ryder to let him know so he can look into it."

Rolling her eyes, she waved her hand. "I'm sure I'm just looking for someone to blame so this can be over." She shot him a playful glance. "I'm more interested in that exchange between you and David?"

Britney Wolf was flighty, not dumb. She had to see what was going on in that exchange David had with Hendrix. "He's making a move on you."

A combination of a scoff and a chuckle popped out. "What? No, he's not."

"Yes, he was."

"Hendrix, I told you he's not interested in me like

that. We're friends. That's all we've been, and that's all we'll be. Even if he was interested in me, I'm not interested in him. He's a great guy, but there's zero spark."

Hendrix flicked his gaze in David's direction and back to Britney. "That doesn't mean he isn't going to try lighting fireworks to make it happen."

"I guess he can try, but I'm a bucket of water where he's concerned. It's not happening." Britney held Hendrix's gaze, a mischievous glint in her eyes. "Besides, I'm saving my sparks for someone else."

"Who?" The question fell from Hendrix's mouth before he could decide if it was a question he should ask or want the answer to.

Leaning forward, she batted her lashes, lifting one shoulder. "Why, Mr. Wells, are you wanting Venus to reveal her secrets?"

This woman. For every push he gave her, she seemed that much more determined to flirt with him. The sad part was that it felt like his heart was a hungry dog begging for whatever she wanted to give him. He could pretend all he wanted. He liked her, and he liked her attention.

"I need to use the restroom. When the waiter returns to take our orders, I'll have the chef's salad and the cheesecake." She stood and stopped next to him, bending at the waist and touching her lips to his cheek. "I'll be back in a second." She winked.

Did the woman have no mercy? No, no she didn't, but it wasn't because she was conceited. She was just... her. He touched the spot where she'd kissed him. Inwardly, he groaned. He was a walking dead man.

9

With her gaze pointed at the floor, Britney grinned as she walked back to her table. She'd had to use the girls' room and asked Hendrix to order for her if the waiter returned.

Hendrix Wells. Oh, he was...he was something else. Adorable. Fun. Hot as Texas asphalt in August, and, boy, did she love to make him blush. She got such a kick out of seeing his grin and the shake of his head.

She bounced off a body and quickly apologized. "Sorry."

Lifting her head, she was greeted by a half-smile from David. "It's okay." He grimaced and waved a hand down his shirt, bringing her attention to a wet spot at center mass. "Kind of wined myself."

Chuckling, she said, "At least it wasn't red wine."

"True. Otherwise, I'd be changing shirts." He laughed. "If I remember right, pizza was your nemesis."

"Just because I manage to drop pizza sauce every time doesn't mean... Fine. Yes. It's awful. It doesn't matter what I do." She made out like she was perturbed.

He tapped her shoulder. "I'm messing with you. It was cute."

She rolled her eyes. "I got your cute."

The air seemed to shift. He chewed his lip a second and then gently took her arm, guiding her closer to the wall. "Could I ask you something?"

It gave her an odd vibe, but she dismissed it. Hendrix was wrong about David. He wasn't interested in her. "Sure."

"That guy you're with...he doesn't really seem your type."

"What do you mean?" She was genuinely curious since it had been so long since they'd spoken. How would David know anything about her *type*?

He leaned his shoulder against the wall as he slipped his hands into his trouser pockets. "I just mean he looks a little rough for you. All the tattoos, the dangerous feel. I swear he was killing me with his eyes. And honestly, I'm almost certain he could if he wanted to."

Part of her wanted to come clean, but she didn't want

to botch the plan. They'd just arrived on the island. There was a good chance that if the stalker was planning to follow her, he'd either yet to arrive or he could be close by and listening. Plus, it gave her an excuse to act like Hendrix's girlfriend. "Rough around the edges maybe, but dangerous? No."

"I get a weird feeling from him." David's lips turned down. "I just don't want to see you get hurt."

"I appreciate that, but he wouldn't hurt me. At least, not on purpose. It's not in his nature." She lowered her gaze to the floor as she pictured Hendrix. "I love his tattoos. Most people carry their baggage on the inside where no one can see it. His is declared like a badge of honor. All those moments captured on his skin document the times he's struggled, what he learned, and his fortitude to keep going." Rolling her lips in, she lifted her gaze. "My mouth kind of went on autopilot. Sorry."

"Sounds like you really care about him." If she didn't know him, she'd think David looked a little disappointed, but he knew where she stood and had for a long time.

"I do, and he made it easy." Easier than anyone she'd ever met. She smiled. "I appreciate the concern, though." She tipped her head in the direction of the dining room. "Guess I should get back."

David straightened. "Sure. Catch you later."

"Okay," she said, continuing back to the dining room. When she reached Hendrix, she ran her hand along his shoulders, dipped enough to kiss his cheek, and said, "Thanks for waiting on me." He was her boyfriend, right? What girlfriend wouldn't want to kiss him?

Eyes wide as saucers stared at her. "Uh, sure. What was that for?" He touched his cheek, swallowing hard.

"Aren't we pretending to date?" She tilted her head, giving him the most innocent look she had. "What girl of yours wouldn't want to have a reason to kiss you all the time?"

His Adam's apple bobbed. "Okay." The word came slowly like he was struggling for it.

She'd rendered him near speechless and suspected she'd been right about women he'd dealt with in the past. He wasn't used to a woman setting her feet and pushing back on that wall he'd erected. "I see the waiter returned. Did you order yet?" She took a sip of her water.

"Uh, yeah, I told him you wanted the salad, and I got the steak and fries."

"With the truffles?" She laughed.

Shaking his head, he shot her a lopsided smile. "No, they can keep that stuff."

"Chicken." The utensils clattered to the table as

she shook out her napkin and laid it in her lap. "I think I'm going for another swim when dinner is over. That nap was probably not a good idea. No matter how much I want to make up for the ones I didn't take as a toddler, all they do is make it harder to sleep at night."

"No way. It'll be too dark."

She lifted an eyebrow. "And you think you're going to stop me?"

He opened and closed his mouth a couple of times. "Yeah, I sure do. I promised I'd keep you safe, and that's exactly what I'm going to do."

"Challenge accepted."

"What?" His jaw dropped. "There's no challenge. Why would you even fight me on this?"

Man, he was cute when he was ruffled. "I'm not. I'm telling you what I'm going to do. You can either come along or sit in the house. I'm in Hawaii, and I'm going to enjoy myself."

Before he could respond, their waiter brought their food out and set it in front of them. Britney closed her eyes as she inhaled. "That steak looks really good." She opened them, pouting. "I think I ordered the wrong thing."

"I'll let you have some if you'll promise to make my job easy."

She locked eyes with him and grinned. “I’m not that hungry.”

He grumbled something under his breath she couldn’t decipher. “Just…just eat your food.”

Inside, she giggled like someone was tickling her. It was as if the universe had picked this darling man out for her. During their meal, they continued to spar, but at some point, he went from being frustrated to amused, or that’s how it seemed to her.

As people finished their meals, one of the band members came to the microphone and opened the floor for dancing. The crowd thawed, and shortly, several couples took them up on the invitation.

Britney leaned in. “Let’s dance.”

“No. I’ve got two left feet.”

“Oh,” she said and sat back. “Well, okay. I’ll go ask David. We need to catch up on stuff anyway.” She waved that red flag and watched the bull paw the ground.

Hendrix’s jaw tightened as he worked it. “Fine. We’ll dance.”

“Do you feel threatened or something? He’s just a friend.”

“I’m not jealous,” Hendrix growled.

This time she couldn’t hold it in, and laughter bubbled out. What an interesting choice of words. “I didn’t say *jealous*.”

His lips pinched together. “You know what I meant.”

“All right. Don’t get so rattled.” She leveled her eyes at him. “He knows I’m here with you. It would just be a harmless dance.”

Pushing out of the chair, Hendrix held out his hand to her. “Would you like to dance or not?”

“You’re entirely too grouchy to dance.” She was testing his patience and she knew it, but this was the most fun she’d had in a long time.

Hendrix inhaled and let it out slowly. “Would you please dance with me?”

Slipping her hand into his, she stood. “I’d be delighted.”

They reached the dance floor, and he slid his arm around her waist, pulling her closer. “I really don’t know how to dance.”

“Maybe it’s not all about the dancing,” she said, flattening her hands against his chest as they began slowly moving. “You sure are muscled, aren’t you?” Under her hands, his heart startled like a spooked thoroughbred, and by the look on his face, he knew she’d felt it. It was all she could do to keep a straight face. “I think I might nickname you Secretariat.”

Hendrix groaned. “Why are you messing with me like this? I mean, I know we need to make it look real, but...”

She batted her lashes. "Sweetheart, you're the one who said we needed to sell this. I'm simply putting on a price tag."

Slowly, a smile lifted his lips. "You are a pain, and you know exactly what you're doing, using those feminine wiles on me."

"Why, Hendrix, are you calling into question my character? I would never stoop to something so low."

A range of emotions clashed in his eyes. "I'm no good for you. If you knew me, *really knew me*, you'd know that," he said, the smile slipping. "I want you to be happy and loved by someone better than me."

Britney slid her hands up his chest and locked her fingers together on the back of his neck. "And if *you* really knew *me*, you wouldn't say that."

His arms tightened around her as he buried his face in her neck. "I don't want to hurt you." The movement of his lips against her skin made butterflies dance in her stomach.

"How about this. Tomorrow is a word we're erasing from our dictionary. We enjoy ourselves while we're on this island, and we leave just like we landed, as friends." She pulled back. "Can we agree on that?"

"All right. Friends. But you need to understand that it's all I can give you."

"That's all I'm asking for. Don't take anything I do

seriously, okay? We've just met, and we're still in the fun, flirty stage." She smiled, lifted on her toes, and kissed his cheek. "Stop worrying and lighten up."

Their little talk seemed to have done just what she wanted. The rigidness in his body eased, and it was like a weight was lifted off his shoulders. A smile formed on his lips. "All right. As long as we understand each other."

"Loud and clear." The words came from her lips with no heart at all behind them.

They danced a little more, and knowing they had an early schedule to keep, they returned to the bungalow. As they reached the steps, she stopped short.

Sitting on the doormat was a pig with its stuffing ripped out, the body mangled by large gashes. Britney covered her mouth with her hand. The stalker *had* followed them to Hawaii. When she'd hatched this plan, she didn't actually think it would happen.

She angled toward Hendrix. "I think I'm a little scared now." For him. "I don't want you to get hurt. I..." Tears pooled in her eyes. "I don't want anyone..." Her voice caught.

He wrapped his arms around her, tucking her head under his chin. "It's going to be okay. I'm not ditching you like those other jerks." He was playing up the ruse, but if he got hurt because of her, she'd never forgive herself.

Bracing her hands on his chest, she leaned back. "But not like this. Not..."

Pulling her close again, he set his lips to her ear. "I know you're scared, but it'll be okay. Let's go inside."

Hendrix slid his arm across her shoulders as they walked up the steps. He picked up the destroyed pig and a note with large black letters that said, *She's mine*.

After they were inside, she hugged herself. "That note isn't for me. None of this is for me. I've put you in danger." She touched her fingers to her lips. "Maybe it hasn't been about me this whole time. Maybe it's been about the guys I've dated."

He shook his head. "You can't make that assumption. The message the drone dropped was for you. This is to warn me, but he's staked claim to you. We still need to be careful."

"I guess."

"Let me check the monitors, all right? Then we'll go from there."

Nodding, she kept her gaze trained on the note. It most certainly wasn't the right time for a relationship. She wasn't even sure she wanted to pretend anymore.

She'd had such a cavalier attitude toward the whole

thing. All of this was her fault, and now Hendrix was the target.

A relationship was out of the question until this stalker was caught. Maybe later, once the stalker was in custody. Then she'd think about it. Putting someone she might love in that sort of danger was wrong and irresponsible. She wasn't that selfish or self-centered. Hendrix said she deserved better. Now, she was thinking he had it all wrong. He was the one who deserved better.

10

"Yeah, there's video of the person sticking the pig and the note on the porch, but it was like they knew there might be cameras. They had on a bulky hood and a facemask. They slouched too, like they wanted to conceal their height." Hendrix would put his fist through their teeth when he found them.

Ryder groaned. "Great."

Hendrix stared at the still video feed. "He's kind of got the build of that David guy. The one Britney knows from high school. She doesn't seem to think he has any interest in her, but he's very...present."

Almost the second she'd left the dining room, David had conveniently spilled wine on himself, and Hendrix had followed him. He'd caught up to them and huddled behind a stack of chairs. Then he'd heard David ask about Britney's relationship, and his feet were glued in place.

Hendrix was warmed head to toe with the way she'd described him. Rough around the edges—she was being gracious. Dangerous, to anyone who might try to hurt her. What grasped his heart the tightest was the way she described his tattoos.

They'd almost sounded noble, the way she spoke. He'd been stunned. No one had ever used language like that when speaking of him. He was a teenage runaway from a horribly twisted family and had turned to a gang to substitute for what he lacked at home. Hearing words like honor and fortitude coming from her lips made his ears ring.

He'd forced himself to truck it back to the table before he made a fool of himself. Then she'd flirted with him mercilessly. He'd loved it, even though he'd had to shut her down.

"Timing does fit, but so far, I'm not seeing anything concrete. All we have is circumstantial." Ryder cleared his throat. "The pizza guy and waiters were all familiar, so that tells me it's someone with similar features. I've got the facial recognition going, though. Maybe it'll turn up something."

"If he is the one doing it, it might be hard. She said

the waiter tonight had a gap in his teeth. You don't have straight teeth one day and gaps the next."

"Unless he's using false teeth. You can order that stuff online now."

"Yeah, I forgot about that. This last threat really upset Britney." Way more than he'd expected. He'd seen fear in her eyes when she looked at him. Her body had trembled as they walked into the bungalow.

That was common, though. One minute, a threat didn't feel real, and the next, it did. He wasn't sure why this one in particular had upset her so much. It was a ruined stuffed pig, just like all the others.

A crash came from the kitchen, startling him. Hendrix stood, strode to his bedroom door, and spotted Britney in the kitchen. "Hey, I need to go. Text me if you get anything."

"I will."

Hendrix ended the call and stuck the phone in his pocket as he walked to the kitchen. "Are you okay?" She'd told him she was going to take a bath to help her relax and then go to bed.

She wiped her nose with a tissue and sniffed. "I'm fine. I was hoping to make something to help me sleep."

"Did I wake you? I didn't think I was being too loud. I'm sorry if I did." Each time he tried to get a look at her face, she'd shift to keep him from seeing her.

As he closed a little more of the distance, she turned her back to him and hugged herself. "Uh, no, you didn't. I'm...just restless tonight, I guess."

"Are you sure?" He leaned a little to the right, hoping to see part of her face.

"I am." She gave him a quick glance over her shoulder. "Just...woke up with an insatiable need for..."

A step erased the rest of the distance. Taking her by the shoulders, he slowly made her face him. Red-rimmed eyes stared back at him. If she'd had any sleep at all, it was minimal. She looked like she'd been crying a while.

Her hand jerked to her face and covered her nose. "I'm fine. Really." Her eyes grew misty as he held her gaze.

"You don't look fine."

Britney's hand dropped to her side to reveal a red-tipped nose. Her lips turned down, and they trembled. "I am," she whispered. He hated that she was so upset.

"We'll catch him. I promise. You're safe for now. I won't let anything happen to you."

Her eyebrows knitted together. "You think that's what's upsetting me? That I might get hurt? I'm worried about you. If something happens to you because of me..." She drew in a shuddering breath. "I'll never be able to forgive myself."

Hendrix could see her being the kind of person who didn't like seeing anyone in danger. He smiled. "He's not going to hurt me."

She balled her fists in his shirt. "You don't know that." Her lips trembled again. "You need to go. I'll be fine here. He's never tried to hurt me. When I get back to Houston, then we'll deal with it."

"It was just another stuffed pig."

"No, it wasn't." She searched his eyes. "It was mangled. They'd ripped the stuffing out. Left a note." The pitch of her voice lifted. "They want to..." Her lips snapped closed. "You should go. You're the one he's targeting."

Him? Leave her there? It wasn't happening. Not just because he promised to keep her safe, but the thought of something happening to her... He couldn't let that happen. He put his arms around her, drawing her closer. "If you want, *we* can go back to Houston."

Pulling away, she shook her head. "I can't."

He knitted his eyebrows together. "Why? I know weddings are a big deal, but Ruby seems like an understanding person. I bet she'd be okay if you had to leave."

She shook her head. "No, I made a promise I'd be in her wedding, and I have to keep it. I just have to. I don't have a choice."

"Can you tell me why?"

Catching his gaze, she stepped closer. "No, I can't. I promised I wouldn't tell."

"Your secrets are safe with me." He smiled.

She palmed his chest and caught his gaze, and he'd never had such intensity staring back at him. "But if I tell you her secrets, it means yours won't be safe with me. That'll mean you can't trust me with yours. I promised I'd never tell a soul, and I won't."

Hendrix stared at her a second. Wow. He'd never heard that response before. "You can tell me, and I'll still trust you."

Her head tilted as her eyebrows knitted together. "Would you, though? You say that, but deep down you know that's not true. If I tell her secret, no secret is safe. This is all or nothing with me." She took a deep breath. "*You* are in danger, and you need to get as far away from me as you can."

"He's been stalking you. You're the one in danger. I'll be fine." He tried putting as much confidence in the words as he could to reassure her.

Her whole body shook with the next inhale. "This whole thing was my idea. I was selfish and self-centered. All because..." She rolled her lips in. "I don't care about myself. This was my stupid idea, and...now you could get hurt. Because of...me."

The second his arms tightened securely around her,

pulling her to his chest, she came undone. He'd had plenty of clients who wept for themselves, but he'd never had anyone this concerned for his safety. Of course, they didn't want him hurt, but it was secondary to themselves. What he felt coming from Britney was a new experience. She was putting his safety—his life—above her own.

He swept her up in his arms and walked to the couch, sitting down with her in his lap. "It's okay. You don't need to cry." That only seemed to make her cry harder.

From that point, he just held her, letting her cry and hoping it was what she needed. He hated that she was so upset, especially over him. One of the reasons he liked the military and working for private security was that he didn't need to be careful. If something happened to him, it was okay. No one was going to miss him.

Until now, it seemed.

The idea that anyone would care that much was new. Most of the time, he took people's word with healthy skepticism. They weren't trying to be dishonest, but it was just human nature to say one thing and do another.

Like his parents. They'd tell him they loved him and then use him to put out their cigarettes. Tell him they were going to the grocery store for food, only to return with drugs. They loved him but didn't mind trading him for drugs when they were short on money. At least he'd been smart enough back then to lock him and his brother in the closet.

Gradually, Britney's cries softened until she was asleep in his arms. It was strange to feel such contentment holding her. She was the one who'd needed comfort, but he was the one who felt peace.

She curled her hands under her chin and snuggled closer. When he ran his fingers through her hair, not only did he find it amazingly soft, but she also sighed and pressed her face harder against his chest. He couldn't piece together why holding her felt so different from previous clients.

His heart had no trouble finding an answer. He was falling for her. Well, fallen. The falling part started the second she walked into the room Friday night. It was like a sunbeam spotlight proclaimed her as *the one.*

Studying her face, he could picture himself happy and content. Holding her, kissing her, being with her. Every time he'd refortified his walls, she'd sashayed through them with a smile. She was an easy woman to like...and want. He'd never felt anything remotely like this about any woman.

He'd slogged through life. Ambivalent was the best way to describe it. He had friends, but they weren't close.

Not enough that he'd ever trust telling them about his past. He'd never told anyone he loved them either. The only time he'd dated someone longer than a few months, part of the reason she'd left him was because he wouldn't say it and never planned *to* say it.

As a little boy, he'd said it to his mom, until she began abusing drugs and him. He'd said it over and over, but it didn't matter. After a while, he learned that love was just a word like any other. It didn't mean anything special.

Britney shifted in his arms, and her eyes opened. A small gasp escaped as she realized what had happened. When she went to move, he held her still. He liked their current situation. "You're okay."

"I fell asleep on you." Her eyes widened. "And used you as a tissue." She covered her face with her hands. "Oh my word. I've never been so embarrassed."

He chuckled. At least he was right in his assessment that caring for someone was messy. "I don't mind." As long as it was her. He pulled her hands from her face and smiled. "Do you feel better?"

"Well, I did." She palmed the side of his face. "You really need to leave. I was absolutely serious about that. Noah could come. I'm sure they know he's my brother."

"And if they don't?"

She chewed her bottom lip. "Yeah, I can't risk that, but you still need to leave. I'll be fine."

If anything happened to her, Hendrix wouldn't be okay ever again. Hugging her to him, he buried his face in her neck. "I'm not leaving you here."

"You're incredibly stubborn, you know that?"

He leaned back. "Me? No way. You take that title."

Her lips pressed into a thin line as fire built in her eyes. "Don't you flirt with me and try to turn it around. You could get hurt."

"I'll take my chances." He yawned and leaned his head back against the couch. "I'm glad the Couple's Quiz is tomorrow instead of surfing. I'm actually kind of looking forward to surfing, and I don't want to be exhausted."

"We don't have to do the quiz. You don't have to do anything you don't want." She sat up a little straighter.

"I know."

Leaning closer, the fire in her eyes a second ago turned to concern. "I'm sorry I kept you up so late."

Touching his fingertips to her temple, he took a deep breath as his fingers traced the side of her face. "I made out all right."

She set her elbow against the cushion next to his face, putting her head in it. With her free hand, she pushed his hair back. "Have I told you how much I like you?" She grinned.

"I might be a little deaf. Wouldn't hurt to say it again." He winked, and his eyes slid closed like he'd snapped the toothpicks keeping them open.

The last thing he heard was Britney telling him good night, and then her lips touched his cheek. It was a good dream to fall asleep to.

11

Britney's heart was still in shambles from the night before. That gutted pig had hit her all kinds of wrong. Yes, it was still just a stuffed animal, and the headless ones were bad, but that one? The gashes? All the stuffing spilling out and then the note.

And none of it meant for her.

It didn't take a mental giant to put together that Hendrix was the one in danger. The stubborn Hulk wouldn't leave, either. As sweet as it was, she still fretted that he'd get hurt and all because she'd been stupid and selfish.

If it were possible, she'd leave as well, but Ruby...the last few years had been horrible for her. Finding Doug had helped her in more ways than one, especially mentally. It was simply a promise Britney couldn't chance breaking.

Yawning, Hendrix quickly covered his mouth with the back of his hand. "Sorry."

"You don't need to apologize. You're tired because of me." She'd managed to wake him enough to get him to bed, and before his head hit the pillow, he was out again. He'd seemed none the wiser when he woke up, either.

He put his arm around her and pulled her legs over his lap. Other couples sitting on the restaurant patio were doing much the same as they waited their turn to take the Couple's Quiz, so it made sense that Hendrix would try to make their relationship look real. "If I have to be tired because of someone, I'd pick you."

Circling her arms around his neck, she touched her forehead to his chin. "Hendrix..."

"Britney, it's okay." He rubbed her back, tightening his hold on her and setting his lips against her ear. "We have cameras, the house has an alarm set, and I have my service weapon. He can't hurt me."

She pulled back. "You are Superman to me, with all your muscles and that sexy smile, but you aren't bulletproof." She brushed her hand against his cheek. "And you're too big to bubble wrap."

He raised an eyebrow. "Sexy smile?"

"That's all you got out of that?" She rolled her eyes. "Really?"

His eyes twinkled as he shot her a smile. He slid his hand up her back, cupped her head, and brought her forehead to his lips. "You are like the best dessert I've ever had, and I'm pretty sure I've found my new favorite way to get sick from overeating."

When he took his hand away, she sat back and leveled her eyes at him. "That charm will not work on me."

"Yeah, it will," he said, holding her gaze.

She huffed.

Chuckling, he said, "My, my, how the tables have turned." The jerk was laughing at her. If only he were wrong. He'd flipped that table like he was Iron Man, and she loved it.

Cocking her jaw, she shook her head. "Just you wait, Mr. Wells. That table's not done turning."

This time his head fell back as he laughed. It was the first time she'd gotten this laugh. So deep and rich and delightful. And she'd done it. What a man.

"Fine. Laugh. What we should be doing is discussing our basics. Favorite color and food and music. Things like that. I hadn't even thought about that until Ruby started asking the others about them," she said. "My favorite color is blue, I love ice cream, and I like country music. How about you?"

"The color of your eyes, French fries, and I like country too."

"Two out of three ain't bad." She laughed. "You like the color of my eyes?" Charmer.

Nodding, he smiled. "You have the brightest, bluest, prettiest eyes I've ever seen." He covered his mouth as he yawned again, setting his forehead on her shoulder. "I need coffee or something."

"A nap?"

He moaned. "A nap."

"Britney and Hendrix?" Ruby called.

Britney took her arms from his neck, held his face, and touched her lips to his cheek. "Let's own this quiz, and then you can take a nap."

For a breath, his gaze darted from her eyes to her lips, like he was in a quandary of what to do. "Nap. Yeah, badly." Just as she stood, he said, "Twenty-two tattoos."

She grinned. Table-turning time. She flicked her gaze down the length of his body. "I think I'll need to count them myself to make sure."

His face fell. Then he rolled his eyes and sighed in frustration.

They walked to the front of the patio and took the hot seats. It was easy to see Hendrix didn't care for the attention. He sat forward like he was preparing to run if he needed to.

Ruby faced the audience. "This is Hendrix Wells and Britney Wolf. Before we get to the questions, tell us how you met."

"We met by way of my brother," Britney said. "We just hit it off."

"Sweet." Ruby looked down at her notes. "The sparks just happened, huh?"

Nodding, Britney hugged Hendrix's arm. "More like lightning." She chuckled.

Hendrix smiled and nodded. "Yep."

It was a show for the audience. Had to be. But then again, he didn't have to agree with her. It made her heart skip a beat.

"All right. Now to the questions." Ruby looked their way and back to the audience. "We'll start with easy ones."

It was a tad embarrassing to get a couple of answers wrong, but they covered well, or so Britney thought, using the fact that they loved to tease each other as the reason.

"Now the hard questions," Ruby said. "Hendrix, what is Britney's biggest insecurity?"

Britney shifted in her seat a little and looked at him. There were plenty to choose from, but which one would he say? She braced herself. Whatever he said, it would be okay. She knew she had weaknesses, with him becoming the biggest ever.

"Her parents went through a horrible divorce brought on by her dad's medical condition. She's afraid that'll happen to her."

Ducking her head, she nodded. "I am." He'd poked his finger into the pothole in her heart. What if the person she chose only wanted her when it was easy? There was no way to test that until it happened.

Ruby shuffled the index cards in her hand. "Britney, is there something in Hendrix's past that he's ashamed of?"

Like she'd answer that. Plastering on her best and bravest smile, she said, "That he didn't meet me long ago."

"Of all my faults, that would be my largest." He put his arm around her, whispering, "I'm sorry."

Rolling her eyes, Ruby huffed. "A real answer."

"That is the real answer. I don't know if you've noticed or not, but I'm kinda wonderful." Her head fell back as she laughed.

"Again, true," he said, chuckling.

Taking a deep breath, Britney sobered. "But seriously, answering that would damage any trust we might share. That isn't a question I'll answer because I'm supposed to protect him." Something she would do with everything in her for the rest of her life. Whether he wanted her or not, she was taking the position of heart guardian.

"That was actually an awesome answer," Ruby said. "And the one I was looking for. The one thing our pre-marriage counselor said was that in a relationship, we need to have each other's back." Ruby tucked the cards under her arm. "Let's give them some love and call the next couple."

Hendrix stood, reached his hand out to her, and waited until her hand was in his before tugging her to her feet. "Ready, my fair lady?"

"Yeah."

Hendrix led her from the patio to a secluded area and stopped. "I'm sorry I answered her. I shouldn't have done that."

She set both of her hands against his chest. "There's truth to it, though."

"That doesn't make it okay. You flinched. I used words like a sword, and you protected me." He took her by the shoulders. "No one has ever done anything like that for me. Not anyone that...I like."

"I enjoy protecting you." She smiled. "It makes me feel needed."

He wrapped his arms around her, pulling her into

the tightest hug she'd ever had, and sighed. "You...you are one spectacular woman. I... Thank you."

Any moment, she expected him to release her, but he just held her. She certainly didn't mind. Being in his arms was heaven on earth. She was safe and warm and happy.

Keeping one arm around her waist, he leaned back, bringing his free hand to her face and brushing his fingertips across her cheek. "You are worthy of *so* much more."

He bent a little closer, his fingers running along her jaw until he reached her chin and set a finger beneath it. "I know I shouldn't, but..."

The soft-spoken words left his lips, and then he touched them to hers with a gentleness unlike any she'd ever known, followed by a sigh that rumbled deep within his chest.

His lips brushed across hers a few times before she melted against him, circling her arms around his neck. He was delicious and his lips a delicacy. So languid and gentle, like he was savoring her. When had that ever happened before? Never. And nothing in her dreams or fantasies could have ever prepared her for the pure euphoria she was experiencing.

Just as he teased her lips to part, he took his hand from her face and set it on the middle of her back, sliding it up until he was cupping the back of her head. Another tease of his lips, and the kiss deepened further, kindling a fire in her she'd thought was dormant. All she needed was a few hundred years of his kisses. Oh, she'd crave more, but that would be a good start.

As the sweet kiss came to an end, she wanted to cry. Her lungs were grateful, but breathing was overrated when it came to Hendrix.

His eyes locked with hers, stormy and pained.

Her heart froze. "Don't you dare squeeze your lemons on that kiss."

"But...I shouldn't have..."

She softened. "Please don't." Desire and desperation coated the words, and she didn't care. "Please."

He held her gaze for what seemed like hours. "Okay."

Hugging him around the neck, she set her lips against his ear. "Thank you."

"I'm not entirely sure I have the strength to say *no* to you anymore."

She chuckled and rolled her lips in before leaning back. "You do realize knowledge is power, right?"

Shaking his head, he curled his arms around her, giving her a gorilla squeeze and kissing the top of her head. Their laughter tapered off, and he set his cheek against her head. "Thank you for inviting me to this."

Her little heart wiggled with glee. She hugged him around the waist, saying, “I’m glad you came.”

They stood there holding each other a few more minutes before he groaned. “I guess we should get some breakfast.”

“I guess so.”

Fall, falling, fallen...with what felt like just a breath between each word. She’d jumped off the cliff willingly and didn’t regret it one bit. He was worth every tear she might shed. And this week would be one for the diary she’d buy when she got home.

12

"You know, for being so early in the morning, it sure is hot and humid." Britney fanned herself with her hand the next morning as they hiked one of the trails not too far from the resort. The wedding party would be stopping at a campground in the middle of the trail, giving people the option of turning around or continuing on.

Hendrix was hot, but it had nothing to do with the weather or the hiking backpack he was wearing. He'd barely slept Sunday night, trying to comfort her, and last night was worse. Every time he closed his eyes, he was kissing Britney.

Nothing had ever been so easy, felt so right, or given as much peace as kissing her. She'd returned his kiss with a matching passion, and it felt like she'd wanted him as much as he wanted her. It had been an incredible experience, and one he was sure couldn't be replicated by another woman. Just thinking about someone else made his stomach turn.

"Hey," she said, tugging on the hem of his shirt. "I don't have any change on me, but if you'll give me an IOU, I can give you a penny for your thoughts when we get back to the resort." She smiled.

These thoughts about her were his until he had more clarity, but he had considered telling her a little about himself, just to test the waters. He was still hearing her voice in his head on why she'd kept Ruby's secret. Him. Britney wanted his trust, and he couldn't come up with a good reason not to tell her. But as much as he enjoyed being with her, his past just wasn't something he was ready to share yet.

"Uh, just trying to figure out who the stalker is," he replied, which wasn't completely false.

"Me too. The pizza guy and those two waiters all seemed familiar, but they're too different to be the same person. It doesn't make sense." She chewed her lip. "And I know you think it could be David, but it's not him. He's a sweet guy, and we've had a platonic relationship since we were in school."

Crossing her arms over her chest, she took a deep breath. "Although…" She waved it off.

He tapped her arm. "Although what?"

"It's just going to make you jealous," she teased.

"I'm not jealous." And even if he was, he wasn't admitting it.

She bumped him with her shoulder and singsonged, "Body language says otherwise."

Grumbling, he shook his head then laughed. "Whatever. Tell me what happened." Hendrix had only caught the part of their conversation about him Sunday during dinner. If it was body language they were using, David's had screamed he wanted Britney.

"The first night we were here, when I went to the restroom during dinner, I was on my way back to the table and we talked a minute. He'd spilled wine on himself and just had to bring up my pizza-sauce problem. Then he started asking questions about us."

Hendrix knew it. "I told you he was interested in you."

"He's not."

"Right." How she couldn't see it was beyond Hendrix, but to be fair, he'd feel that way about any man who met her. "What sort of questions did he ask?" Would she lie?

"He just said...you didn't seem my type. That you were..." She dropped her hands to her sides. "He said you looked rough and dangerous."

"As much as I hate to agree with the guy..." It went beyond hate for Hendrix.

Britney pulled him to a stop. "He doesn't know you, and I don't think that at all." She caught his gaze as she faced him. "I...like you just the way you are. All your tattoos and edges and everything." She dropped her gaze to the ground and shrugged. "If any of the choices you made in the past were any different, there's a chance I would never have met you." She lifted her head and locked eyes with him. "And I'd be the one poorer for not knowing you."

When she put it in those terms, of them not meeting, Hendrix found himself immensely grateful for the choices he'd made. Not completely, not the worst offenses for sure, but now he had a comparison between life before and life after Britney. The longer he was in her orbit, the deeper his desire grew to remain there, which he knew wasn't possible.

He shook his head. "You may think that, but..."

She took his face in her hands. "Hendrix, listen to me. I don't care. I don't care if you tell me. Nothing will change if you do decide to tell me. You have to know me well enough by now to know that. Don't you?"

He believed that she believed it. Reality was way different. Taking her hands from his face, he pulled her into an embrace. "I know."

Britney inhaled, holding her breath a moment, and slowly let it out. “The longer you hold me, the less I care about how hot and humid it is.”

A sentiment they shared. He could hold her indefinitely and be completely fine. He leaned back and brushed away a few pieces of loose hair framing her face. She was as beautiful on the inside as she was on the outside. And kissable. Those lips beckoned to be kissed, but he’d promised himself he wouldn’t again. Another, and he wasn’t sure he could walk away at the end of the week.

She lifted on her toes and pressed her lips to his, holding them there, and it may as well have been flint being struck against steel. The flame sparked in the pit of his stomach, spreading so rapidly he couldn’t stop himself from responding. He wanted more of her...all of her.

Her arms circled around his neck as he picked her up by the waist and deepened the kiss. Her tiny moan added fuel to the fire racing through his blood. He couldn’t hold her tight enough or kiss her long enough to quench the growing need to be with her.

The kiss the day before was soft and sweet, and this one felt more like an out-of-control blaze. She slid her hands up his neck and buried them in his hair just as her lips left his to brush along his jaw with soft, intermittent kisses. "I like kissing you." Each word punctuated the touch of her lips and her hot breath tickling his skin.

When he couldn't take the tease any longer, he rested his hand against the back of her neck and ran his thumb along her jaw, tipping her head back and running his tongue along her throat, tasting her. With a gasp, she held on to him harder and whimpered.

In that moment, he knew he was ruined. He belonged to her no matter how they left the island. His heart was in the palm of her hands, confession of past sins or not.

Just as he brought his lips back to hers, the clearing of a throat broke through the moment, and Britney startled. Hendrix's lungs screamed, and he felt dazed as he set her feet on the ground.

"Uh, we thought we'd lost you. Um..." the person said. "Um, we'll see you at the campground." Their feet faded as they retreated.

A slow smile lifted Britney's lips as she lifted on her toes, kissing him again. "If you say one negative—"

He cut her off with another kiss. "There aren't any, but—"

Britney covered his mouth with her hand. "Promise me something."

Taking her hand from his mouth, he asked, "Like

what?" Not that it mattered. If she wanted it and he could do it, it was hers.

Her eyebrows knitted together as she held his gaze. "Promise me first."

The only person he'd ever done that for was the man who'd seen something in him worth saving. "I've only done that for one person in my life."

"I'm very curious as to who that could be, but if you never tell me, I won't care. I just want...a little promise. One that will only remain valid on this island."

"You have my promise. As long as it doesn't include streaking or karaoke. Or leaving the island without you coming with me."

"Okay." She blinked and shook her head. "Wait. What? Streaking or karaoke? Those seem out of the blue and very specific."

He chuckled. "I haven't done either and plan to go to my grave that way."

Her eyes narrowed a second. "I believe you."

She did? "Really? Why?"

Shrugging, she smiled. "I have no reason not to."

"What's the promise?" he asked, wondering what she could possibly want from him.

Her eyes darkened for just a flash, and she waved him off and began walking. "Never mind. It's stupid."

With a stride, he caught up. "Now I'm very curious. What promise do you want?"

"Really, it's okay. My mouth was running faster than my brain. It's…it's okay."

Pulling her to a stop, he said, "Tell me."

When she wouldn't meet his gaze, he set a finger under her chin and lifted her head until their eyes locked. "What?"

"I'm not very good at making people keep their promises, and it's pathetic and embarrassing and…if you say no…" She groaned. Taking her lip between her teeth, she brought her gaze back to his. "Do you think you could be mine for the rest of this week?"

His jaw dropped. Hers? He didn't know how to respond. Of course, his heart was panting like a dog, but his brain was giving him painful flashes of the future where she wasn't in his life.

Although, there was the issue of the stalker. Maybe she was just playing it up, thinking they'd been followed. That wouldn't make sense, though. If anything, her request would have made the stalker aware that they'd been faking it.

The debate was giving him a headache. If she needed his promise, she had it. If nothing else, he'd have the remainder of the trip to be hers. Which meant she'd be his. And he'd never wanted anyone more than he wanted her.

"See, it was stupid." Groaning, she pulled away and began walking again. "Just don't worry about it."

She'd put enough distance between them that by the time he gathered his wits, he had to jog to catch up with her. He took her by the arm and made her face him. "I'm yours."

"Really?" Her eyes lit up much like a kid who'd asked for the impossible Christmas gift.

Hendrix wasn't sure what shocked him more, that she wanted him or that she was shocked he'd agreed. No one had ever wanted him. They'd wanted something from him, but not *him*. "Yeah."

She threw her arms around his neck, nearly choking him. "Thank you."

She leaned back. "You aren't just saying that because I made you promise, are you? I don't want that. I don't want to—"

He cut her off with a kiss. Obviously, she didn't understand how powerful a pull she had. The next few days would only be a blink, but he'd savor every second he had with her.

Shouts from a few feet up the trail spoiled the moment, and Britney grumbled, "This trek has been hot, humid, and now frustrating. We're on a romantic island. You'd think they'd catch a clue."

"We could go swimming when we get back to the bungalow," he said, giving her a quick kiss before releasing her.

She twined her fingers with his and smiled. "That sounds good to me."

Once they reached the campsite, they staked out a spot to sit where Hendrix shrugged out of the backpack he'd worn. He pulled out two brown bags, handing one to Britney and then passing her a water bottle.

Twisting off the cap, she tipped it up and drained it halfway before gasping for air. "Oh, it's tepid, but, man, it tastes good."

He finished off his and nodded. "I'm glad I brought a few."

Her stomach growled, and she slapped her hand over it. "You'd think it's been forever since I've eaten. Honestly, I didn't think I'd be that hungry when we left, but I think I could eat leather right now."

"I feel like I should have asked for a second sandwich." He unscrewed the cap off another water bottle and took a big drink.

Britney opened her bag and wrinkled her nose. "Ham? When I ordered it, it sounded great. Now, not so much."

"We can trade if you want. I think this one is turkey, but a sandwich is a sandwich to me. You want to switch?"

She sagged. "Are you sure?"

"Go ahead. I like ham just as much."

"Thanks," she said as they swapped food.

"You're welcome." He took a giant bite. It was delicious with a hint of pineapple flavoring. "This is pretty good."

Britney tore off a piece of the turkey. "This is too. It's not dry like some of them." She looked around. "It sure is pretty here, but I think I like the beach more."

Ruby walked to the middle of the campsite and waited for everyone to quiet down. "Once you're finished eating, you're free to go a little farther on the trail, or you can head back to the resort. There's nothing else planned for today. Tomorrow is snorkeling, and I'm told it's amazingly fun." She glanced at Doug. "We want to thank you again for being in the wedding."

Hendrix finished the last bite of his food and washed it down with a large gulp of water. "Do you want to head back to the resort?"

"I'm okay with whatever you want to do. If you want to hike some more, we can."

"I think the beach is calling to me."

She eyed him. "Is it, or are you just saying that because I prefer it?"

"I like the beach." He grinned. "It's way more fun to toss you than it is to hike."

"Okay, but remember, I may not be able to pick you up, but I have other ways of getting you back."

"Totally worth it." He chuckled.

Her frustrated sigh and roll of the eyes only made it funnier. He knew he'd pay later, but in a way, he actually looked forward to whatever she tried.

Finished with her food, she stuffed the trash in the paper sack and drained her bottle of water. "All right, tough guy, let me tell Ruby, and we can go back to the resort."

Britney stood and walked to Ruby, who was engaged in a conversation with one of the other bridesmaids. They took turns hugging each other. After talking a minute, Britney looked at Hendrix and then returned her attention to Ruby and company. Was he the topic of conversation, and what was being said?

One more hug, and Britney returned to Hendrix, rocking back on her feet. "Okay, ready."

He looked up at her. "Were you talking about me?"

"Maybe." She grinned.

"About what?"

She tapped him on the nose. "Secrets, Mr. Wells. I'm

a wealth of mystery and secrets," she said with a wink and then sashayed to the mouth of the trail leading back to the resort.

His mouth went dry. He wasn't opposed to treasure hunting where Britney was concerned.

Taking a large drink of water, he scrambled to stuff their trash into the backpack before jogging to catch up with her. "What sort of secrets?"

"Oh, sweetheart, if I tell you, it won't be a secret." She shrugged and gave him the sexiest, sultriest smile he'd ever seen. "And that's just no fun."

He stopped, looked heavenward, and let out a frustrated groan. Her return came in the form of a throaty laugh that only made her that much sexier.

Again, he jogged to catch up with her. "I don't know why it's fun to you."

She spun on her heels and began walking backward. "I like the blush on your cheeks. The way you smile when you're frustrated and you don't know what to say. Almost like a woman has never teased you."

"I don't smile." Or he didn't think so.

"It's small, but the corners of your lips turn up. I doubt you even realize it. And then there's that," she said, wiggling her finger at his eyes. "They twinkle, and I love it."

"I don't do any of that."

"Yeah, they—" She stopped midstride and held her stomach, swallowing hard.

"You okay?"

Waving him off, she turned and began walking again. "Yeah, I'm fine." The sentence was barely out of her mouth before she bent at the waist and braced her hands on her knees. "Maybe…maybe I'm…" She inhaled and exhaled a few times.

"What's going on?" His gaze roamed over her body, trying to figure out what was wrong.

She held up a finger and then dashed into the foliage before throwing up. By the time Hendrix reached her, she had one hand against a tree and the other holding her stomach. Over and over, she emptied the contents of her stomach until she was dry heaving.

"Could I have some water?" she asked when she finally had a break.

"Yeah," he replied, grabbing the bottle he'd tucked in his pants pocket for later. He twisted off the cap and handed it to her.

As she rinsed her mouth, she swayed. "I'm dizzy all of a sudden."

Hendrix closed the distance, wrapping his arm around her to steady her. In what felt like a heartbeat, she'd gone from fine to pale and pasty. There had only been one time prior to this that Hendrix had witnessed something similar, and it involved drugs. He pulled out his phone and dialed 9-1-1. "I think we need to get you to the hospital."

"It's probably...just..." The last word slipped out barely above a whisper, and her knees buckled.

"Hold on, sweetheart. I'm getting help."

As soon as he was done speaking with the operator, he fired off a quick text to her brother, swept her up into his arms, and returned to the trail.

Hopefully, Hendrix's quick response would give them enough time to figure out what was in her system. Maybe that would help them track down whoever might have done it.

13

A hospital. Britney was barely awake, and she knew it. Between the funky soap smell and machine noises, it was a dead giveaway. She opened her eyes and grunted in displeasure. Yep, she was right, and even with the shades down, she could tell it was close to sunset.

"Hey," Hendrix said as the mattress moved and his face came into focus.

Her entire body ached from whatever had hit her. "Hi."

Brushing her hair back, he smiled. "How are you feeling?"

"Like I have a sadistic yoga instructor." She grunted a laugh, regretting it as the muscles in her stomach protested. “What happened? I remember having an upset stomach and being dizzy, but that’s about it.”

“Honestly, we don’t know yet. They took blood samples, but those take a little time to test. It could have been food poisoning, but Noah, Ryder, and Jax flew in.”

She narrowed her eyes. “Why would they fly in if it was just food poisoning?”

“Well, for one, he’s your brother and he runs a security business. Everything is suspicious right now.” Hendrix brushed her hair from her face. “He just wants to make sure it was actually food poisoning.”

“If it isn’t, what could it be?”

Shaking his head, he replied, “You don’t need to worry about that right now. You just need to rest.”

That was bodyguard speak for something happened and he didn’t want to upset her. “What aren’t you telling me?”

“For now, nothing.”

“But you do have an idea. I can hear it in your voice, and, sure, Noah is protective, but he wouldn’t be here if the two of you didn’t think something else was going on.” She used her arm without the IV needle and pushed herself into a sitting position.

He took her by the arms. “Slow down. It’s okay.”

It didn’t take a math whiz to figure out one plus one. Another option aside from food poisoning was a food allergy, and she didn't have any that she was aware of. Drugs were the only other possibility.

With a gasp, she said, "You. It was meant for you. I was right. I'm not the target; you are." She'd pitched him into the middle of the situation without even considering that it could become dangerous. How could she have been so thoughtless? "If you leave, he'll back off. I can fly home after the wedding, and we can come up with a plan there. One that won't put anyone in his crosshairs."

"I'm not leaving you here unprotected, and if it's true, then I'm already the target. I may as well see this through." He drew her closer, kissing her forehead. "Besides, I really want to take surfing lessons."

She balled her fists into his shirt. "This isn't funny to me, Hendrix. I treated this like a game, and it isn't. I should have said something at the very beginning."

His lips lifted just a fraction as he caught her gaze. "And if you had, I wouldn't have met you."

"And your life wouldn't be at risk."

He took one arm from around her and brushed his fingers along her temple. "You seem to be under the delusion that you aren't worth the risk."

She groaned. "Stop being sweet. I can't stay determined to make you go home when you say things like that."

Laying her back against the bed, he pressed another kiss to her forehead. “I’m going to go get you something to eat and drink. While I’m gone, you need to call your mom. She was pretty upset, and since we’re trying not to bring attention to this any more than we already have, Noah asked her to stay in Houston.”

“All right, but this discussion isn’t over. It’s just on pause.”

Setting his cheek against hers, he said, “I’ve never felt so helpless in my life. You were fine one second, and the next, you were going limp in my arms.” His breath hit her skin, sending shivers down her spine. Leaning back, he smiled. “Phone’s on the nightstand. Call your mom. I’ll be back in a little bit.” With that, he was crossing the room and out the door, shutting it behind him.

What was she going to do with him? She grabbed her phone and dialed her mom. “Hey,” she said as the line picked up.

“Oh, sweetheart, I’m so glad to hear your voice. How are you feeling?”

“Sore from throwing up and a little tired still, but otherwise, I’m fine.” Britney held her stomach as she slouched down a little more in the bed.

Her mom gave a sigh of relief. “Thank goodness. Noah said they don’t know what happened yet. He hinted it could be more than food poisoning, but he said the tests could take up to a day to get back, maybe longer."

"Yeah, that's what Hendrix told me." Britney picked at her blanket. "Mom, I switched food with him. If it's more than food poisoning, it means the stalker is targeting him. It means he could get really hurt because it's moved past just stuffed pigs."

"If. That's a pretty big word for only being two letters. Let the tests come back before you begin fretting. Either way, it wasn't your fault. Hendrix knows what the job entails, and he wouldn't work for Noah if he weren't good at it."

Easier said than done. "Mom..."

"You have feelings for him."

With a groan, Britney turned to her side, facing the window. "Yes. I don't know what it is about him, but the thought that something could happen to him shakes me to the core. I met him Friday. Late night at that. It's not even a week later, and I can't imagine life without him."

Her mom laughed. "The Wolf curse, huh?"

"Seems so. I thought it had skipped me, but I guess I was wrong."

"The second I met your dad, I knew."

Britney grinned. "He said the same thing. You and Dad double-whammied us."

She barked with laughter. "I'm sorry, but, yeah, I'm afraid so."

"He says that if I knew more about him, I wouldn't be interested. I don't know what to do to make him understand I don't care."

After a long pause, her mom said, "You can't make him understand. That's just not something you can force. It will take a heart change from him, because he's got to be willing to take the risk. You can't be the only one in the relationship doing it. It would be way too heavy for you to bear alone. Without sharing that, you'll grow weary, and it'll fail."

"I know, Momma. I just needed to hear you say it. It hurts to think I would have to walk away, but I'm smart enough to know that it takes two." She sighed. "But I don't give up on people easily, so we'll see what happens. I think he's worth it."

"Then he's worth it." Her mom chuckled.

A knock came from Britney's door, and she glanced over her shoulder. "I think Hendrix is back with something for me to eat."

"All right. I'll let you go. Thanks for calling me, honey."

"Love you, Momma." Britney ended the call and rolled to her back. "Come on in."

The door opened, and David stepped inside. "Hey, Ruby said you got sick on the hike. Are you okay?"

He wasn't the man she was expecting at all. "Yeah, I'm fine."

Slipping his hands into his pockets, he walked to her bed and stopped. "Ruby said to tell you she's sorry she can't come. She's got a cake emergency. Apparently, the cooler broke and her cake is in bad shape."

"Oh, it's okay. It was just a bug or something. Add dehydration and, *boom*, hospital stay." She smiled.

His gaze locked with hers. "At least that's all it was." The words sounded innocent enough, but there was a vibe coming from him that she'd never felt before, like he was searching for a way to broach an uncomfortable topic.

Silence stretched for a second, and it was enough to make it uncomfortable. Maybe Hendrix had been right and David thought there was a chance. How conceited would it be to assume that, though, when she was there with someone?

"How has your vacation been so far? Meet anyone promising?" Not exactly subtle, but she really didn't want to use a club on him if she didn't have to. Plus, if the stalker was around, she couldn't risk the chance of messing up the plan.

Shaking his head, he broke eye contact and said, "It's

been great, but, no, I haven't connected or even really talked with anyone. No one besides you, anyway. This is the first chance I've been able to slow down enough to even think about that." He flicked his gaze to hers and back to the floor. "I'm surprised Hendrix isn't here."

David was about to meet her pricklier side. "He is. He went to get me something to eat, and knowing him, he's having trouble deciding what to get since it's food that put me in here."

"Ah, gotcha. I just thought..." David scratched the back of his neck. "Ruby seemed to imply that you and Hendrix haven't been dating for very long...and I thought maybe we..."

Ruby? Britney couldn't see her friend saying anything like that at all. "If I've sent mixed messages in any way, I apologize profusely. I didn't mean to cause any confusion."

"It's okay."

"No, it's not, and I'm sorry. If I'd even suspected you thought something could happen between us, I would've been more careful. I sincerely apologize." She touched his arm and caught David's gaze. She'd have to apologize to Hendrix too since she'd dismissed the idea that David was making moves on her. "My heart belongs to him. I don't know what the future may hold, but all my visions include him. I can't express properly how much I care for him."

After a few seconds, David's eyebrows knitted together, and he nodded. "The guy just doesn't seem your type. I mean, he's not exactly the kind to run in our circles, you know? When I put it with what Ruby suggested, I guess...I guess I just thought he was a novelty and your relationship wasn't serious. That you were just lonely and he was an available plus-one."

Tears pooled in her eyes. She'd called this man a friend for years, and this is what he thought of her? "What a horrible thing to say. You really think I'd be like that?"

"Hey, I—" Hendrix's words died as he stopped just inside the door. His eyes narrowed just a fraction. "Hi."

"Hi. I was only here for a short visit." David stepped back and seemed to fumble for words. "Uh, I'll get going so you can eat." He reached the door and stopped. "I shouldn't have said that. I...I'm sorry."

"Yeah, that was a sorry thing to say." She blinked back tears threatening to spill.

Hendrix turned to him. "What exactly did you say that you need to apologize for?" The sharp tone made David shrink back.

"Something stupid. I'm really sorry, Britney," he said and rushed out the door.

"What did he say?" Hendrix asked as he strode to the table next to the bed and set the food tray on it.

"Nothing important." She lifted her head and looked away, still working to keep from crying. "I think I made him mad, and he lashed out. That's all."

The bed moved, and Hendrix braced his hand on the bed, leaning across her. "*What* did he say?"

"That...that he thought you were a novelty." Britney pinched her lips together as hurt turned to fury. At David and at herself. "That rat thought I was so shallow as to be like that." She looked at Hendrix. "I don't know what makes me angrier, that he'd accuse me of that or that he'd think so little of you."

No, she knew which one. The very next time she saw David, she was going to tear him up. She didn't care if they were alone or in the middle of a Kline's dress sale; he was getting a tongue whooping. That's if Hendrix didn't pound him first, and by the look in his eyes, that was a good possibility.

"From the bottom of my heart, I didn't think he was making moves on me, but I should have listened to you. I'm sorry." Sitting up on her knees, she hugged Hendrix around the neck. "I know we're just friends, but I'd pick you any day over that pompous jerk."

For a second, he froze, and then he melted against her. "He's probably better for you than I am."

Britney leaned back enough to look him in the eyes. "I know you're twice my size, but you say something like that again, and I'm going to show you just how feisty I can be."

"I might do it just to see what happens." His lips curved into a delicious smile.

This fake relationship had quickly become anything but. At least for her. Hendrix hadn't wanted to come on the trip, and for all she knew, he was still playing a part.

Her mom was right. Noah wouldn't have hired Hendrix if he weren't good at his job. She wasn't sure if he was still pretending or not, and when he added that to her mom's advice, it was a good fortifier for taking things slow. He needed to walk toward her willingly. For now, she'd enjoy her time with him and see where it went.

14

Another restless night. Hendrix swung his feet over the side of the bed early Thursday morning and sat up, raking his hand through his hair. He checked the time on his phone and groaned. It was two in the morning, and the surfing lessons were starting at nine. He'd been looking forward to that since the schedule came out, but with such little sleep since the trip started, he was exhausted. They'd missed out on snorkeling since Britney had to stay at the hospital overnight on Tuesday and most of the following day, and he didn't want to be the reason they missed another activity, especially when it was something he wanted to do.

It didn't help that every time he shut his eyes, he was kissing Britney. There were a few dreams of punching that David guy in the face because the jerk had made her cry. Hendrix had to admit it was cute how mad she got. There was the question of his sanity when he thought it would be fun to see her get really mad.

Scrubbing his face, he wondered if a little fresh air would help clear his mind, and maybe he could catch a few winks before the alarm went off. He walked to the bedroom door and stopped. What was Britney doing on the sofa? And it wasn't even really big enough to be all that comfortable. Not a mark against the resort. Who came to Hawaii to spend their time inside?

Then he caught sight of a...frying pan in her hand? He'd seen his share of a lot of odd things, but this made him set his bar a little higher for next time. He shook his head and leaned against the doorframe, causing the doorknob to smack against the wall.

Britney bolted up, held the frying pan out like a baseball bat, and said, "I'll so hit you with this."

"It's just me."

She startled and hugged the pan to her chest. Even with the little bit of moonlight, he could see her cheeks turning crimson. "Oh. Uh..."

He pushed off the frame and walked to the nearest lamp, switching it on. "Do you normally sleep with a frying pan?"

Turning her back to him, she said, "Well, wouldn't it

make sense to be sleeping with one now that I was poisoned? If the person breaks in, I can whack him."

It was a good argument, but... "Right, and if you'd done that after the gutted pig, I might have bought it, but this is new."

"All right, fine. It occurred to me that if it was more than food poisoning, then that means it was meant for you. I don't want you to—" She faced him, and her eyes went wide.

That's when he realized he'd walked out of his room in just pajama pants. All his tattoos were on display. He slapped his hand over his chest. "Hold that thought." He'd never forgotten to wear a shirt before when sharing space with someone.

He turned, and the next thing he knew, she had her arms around him with her hands flat against his stomach, pressing her cheek into his back. "Please don't shut me out. I promise that all of you is safe with me."

Fire flicked his skin everywhere she touched, and the intimacy of the moment was doing things to his mind and body that he couldn't handle, or at least handle responsibly. Maybe an offer to tell the story of one of his tattoos would give him the space to think, and the chance to see how she'd handle it. "One. I'll tell you about one tattoo." It was the bravest offer he'd ever made, but whatever she picked, he'd tell her about it, even a hard one.

"That means I get to count them, right?" Still plastered against his back, she laughed, and it danced across his nerves. This woman.

Rolling his eyes, he twisted in her arms. "You don't fight fair."

"I can't pick you up and pitch you in the water. I'm simply using what I've got to even the playing field." She grinned and batted her lashes at him.

He exhaled heavily. "Just pick one."

"All right, Mr. Grumpy Pants. Just give me a second," she said, putting a little space between them. Her gaze floated from one side of his torso to the other and top to bottom. Then she slowly walked around him. Her finger came to rest on his skin, tracing one tattoo after the other.

Without lifting her finger from his skin, she stopped at his arm until he held it up so she could continue around him. She looked up, brushed her thumb across a tattoo on the underside of his arm, seeming to inspect it. If she kept that up much longer, he'd jump out of his skin. Her touch was fraying what was left of his nerves.

Finally, she faced him and drew an invisible circle around the simplest piece, a two-word statement written over his heart: *I promise*. "That one."

It made no sense. She had her choice. There were plenty that held deeper meanings, even a few that would have been agonizing to talk about. And she'd picked that one? "You could have picked any one of them. Why that one?"

"Because I could hear it in your voice that you wanted to tell me, and at the same time, you were afraid. It's a test of whether you can trust me or not." She covered the small tattoo with her hand. "I'd rather have your trust than your secrets."

His heart thrummed in his ears as he swallowed hard. He'd never met another soul with the ability to read him as well as she could. "It's to remind me to keep my word. That when I say those two words, it's more than just a promise. It's a covenant between me and whoever might be in charge of the world that I'll do what I said, whether I like it or not. There are no take-backs."

She held his gaze, and her lips lifted in a sweet smile before kissing his cheek. "Thank you." Then she turned and walked back to the couch, setting the frying pan in her lap. "I promise too."

He stood there, speechless. Every time he expected her to be like everyone else, she surprised him. He'd stick to the plan and test her, but so far, she was passing with flying colors. "Now, back to your frying-pan thing."

"I don't want you to get hurt. I thought if the person poisoned you, then maybe they'd try something worse." She gave a small shrug. "You came on this trip with me, and we're a team. We're supposed to look out for each other."

The restraint it took not to smile was almost more than he could bear. "You know I have a gun, right?"

"Well, yeah, now that you're bringing it up. At the time, I was just..." She stopped and pulled her hair across her cheek to hide her face from him. "I just wanted to keep you safe."

So far, her ability to surprise him had surpassed every person he'd ever met. "That's perhaps the sweetest thing anyone has ever done for me."

She used the heel of her hand to wipe her face. "It was silly, and it's just like me to not think about you having a gun."

He crossed the small space and sat on the couch. "Not silly at all to me, and I wasn't kidding. It means more to me than you'll ever realize." He leaned forward, trying to look at her, and she twisted away a little more. "You really don't like people seeing you cry, do you?"

Shaking her head, she said, "No, there's enough sadness in the world. I want to be the person people come to when they can't handle things."

How had he been so lucky to meet her? It didn't

make sense. He'd made so many mistakes, and yet he was sitting next to the most amazing woman he'd ever met. A beautiful, bright woman with a strength akin to Atlas. "Who do you go to, though?"

"Sometimes, I'll talk to my mom, but my problems are insignificant compared to others. I just slap a smile on and figure out a way to make things work." She wiped her face again.

He touched her shoulder, and she popped his hand. "I'm not turning you into a tissue again. You don't even have a shirt on. That would be beyond disgusting. I'm still so mortified from the last time that it'll last me forever."

This time he slipped his arm around her shoulders and gathered her to him. "Your problems aren't insignificant to me." Then he wrapped his other arm around her and pressed her against him. "I'll happily take whatever form you need me to be."

"If you make me cry any more, I'll hit you with my frying pan."

The statement hit him as funny, and his head fell back as he laughed. He couldn't recall a time when he'd laughed harder. Maybe as a kid, but he'd had to grow up so quickly that he had no memory of it.

She pressed her hand against him and pulled back. "You're laughing at me."

"Well, yeah, you're threatening me with a frying pan, and you don't have a mean bone in your body."

She scoffed. "I can so be mean."

"No, I don't think you can. You're kind to a fault. You see the good in people when they don't deserve it. You're...incredible." Never had he wanted someone as much as he wanted her.

"If you put me on a pedestal, the only direction I can go is down. I'm imperfect just like every other person on this earth." Her shoulders sagged. "What if I can't live up to your expectations? Will you walk away?"

"I guess I never thought about it like that." She was right, though. He expected perfection from people while using his own past to excuse his actions. "I'm sorry."

Her lips quirked up. "No reason to apologize. We're human. Mistakes come with the journey." She ran her thumb under one of his eyes. "And you're exhausted. You need to get some sleep so you aren't snoozing through those surfing lessons you've been looking forward to."

"I'd argue, but I don't think you'd buy it."

"I wouldn't," she said and stood, taking his hand and pulling him from the couch. "C'mon, you need sleep."

He had to admit, if he was going to be led to bed, she was the one he wanted in charge, and that didn't apply to just the current trip.

As he sat down hard on the edge of his bed, he covered his mouth as he yawned. A second later, she was standing in front of him with a shirt held out.

"I thought you wanted to count my tattoos," he teased and slipped the shirt over his head.

Holding his gaze, she slid her fingers through his hair. "I know I tease you a lot, but I don't want anything of yours that I have to steal. It would mean nothing. The only way it'll mean anything to me at all is if you share it willingly." Bending at the waist, she pressed a soft kiss to his lips. "Get some sleep, Mr. Wells."

"Kisses don't make me sleepy."

She stopped at the door, looked over her shoulder, and delivered the ultimate sultry smile. "Maybe one day we'll explore what *does* make you sleepy," she said, her voice husky.

His pulse rocketed. "That helps even less."

"Goodnight."

With a huff, he flopped back on the bed with his arms spread wide. This woman was going to be the death of him. He wanted her in ways he'd never wanted anyone before. He loved her mind, her wit, the way she walked, the way she talked. It was as though she'd been purposefully designed just for him. Boxes upon boxes were being checked to the point that his future was being planned with a Mrs. he'd never expected to have.

He was a one-man show. Single. Bachelor. The words lit up in his head and slowly dulled into wanted, needed, couldn't live without. The tightrope was now razor-thin, and he was all out of balance.

15

A half-dozen splats in the ocean were enough for Britney to call surfing a no-go. On sand, she was a pro, but once water got involved, she was over it, or, well, in it. Another reason she wasn't brokenhearted she'd missed snorkeling. It was okay but not her idea of fun. She was much better at party planning.

Hendrix, though...he loved it. He'd caught on quickly, as if the talent were innate. He was a beautiful man, too. The shirt and swim shorts made his skin tone look even darker. From the top of his dark hair to the tip of his toes, he was just a hunk. When he was happy, it made it easy for her to envision parking for an eternity just to watch him.

"Hey," Ruby said as she sat next to Britney under the umbrella shade. "Are you feeling better?"

The official story was that she'd reacted to something in the turkey's seasoning. With the resort opening soon, saying it was food poisoning would have hurt Ruby's uncle, and Britney didn't want that, especially if it didn't turn out to be that. If it was foul play, it needed to lie at the stalker's feet.

Noah had dropped by the hospital just before she was released the day before. They were waiting on a call about the blood test to confirm whether it was food poisoning or not. Ryder and Noah were still going through footage, and a member of the resort management had reached out to Noah because a staff member had come to them with some information. Jax was pursuing that lead, and he'd not checked in yet.

"A lot better. I won't be eating whatever they seasoned that turkey with ever again." Truth be told, turkey was off the menu for a while. Going down, it was great. The Texas goodbye, she could have done without.

Ruby hugged Britney around the shoulders. "You're one of my best friends. I feel terrible because I haven't spent the time with you that I've wanted to. Even worse for not coming to the hospital. I'm glad David was able to visit."

Britney would keep that little exchange to herself. He'd apologized, but she wasn't in the forgiving stage yet. That wasn't on Ruby, though, and if she found out, David would be saying goodbye to Hawaii because Ruby wouldn't put up with that nonsense. The gracious part of Britney, a minuscule voice at the moment, wondered if he'd taken offense at what she said. It had been a little bold, but she'd just had a feeling she needed to set him straight.

Hugging her, Britney said, "You've got a dozen people and a wedding you're dealing with. Add a cake disaster, and it's just pandemonium. We're square as square can be. We can talk after your honeymoon. Weekly pedicure is still on, right?"

"Absolutely." Ruby laughed and released Britney. "Did you talk to your mom?"

"If I hadn't, I'd be sandwiched between the two of you right now." She laughed. "She'll be flying in Friday evening for the wedding Saturday."

Ruby smiled. "That makes me happy. I can just imagine your mom with mine and the stories they'd be telling. We'd both be embarrassed forever."

Britney hooked her arm around her friend's shoulders. "Your mom would be so happy for you and proud of you. She'd approve of Doug."

The previous year, Ruby had lost her parents and her youngest sister in a boating accident. Her older sister had taken it hard, but not nearly as hard as Ruby. It had taken months for her to come out of the grief, and even longer for Britney to trust that she could be left alone. Having lost her dad, although not as suddenly, Britney understood her friend's aching heart. No one needed to go through that alone.

"Thanks, Britney."

"Anytime."

Leaning in, Ruby said, "I have to say, Hendrix is so cute. He looks like he's having a blast."

It was a contrast to how he'd seemed that morning. Not that he was in a bad mood, exactly, but it had seemed like he had a lot on his mind. Britney was sure it hadn't helped his sleep, but he'd been determined to take the lessons anyway.

Oh, she'd made such an idiot of herself the night before. A frying pan? What a dopey idea. He had a gun, for crying out loud. After telling him she was going to bed that night, she'd lain there thinking of a million scenarios of him getting hurt, and the worry had driven her to do something, anything, to try to keep him safe.

Then all that talk about her being incredible and stuff. He just didn't understand the pressure that put on her. She wasn't perfect, and the way he painted her made it seem as though he thought she was. How on earth was she supposed to live up to that? How could anyone? She was just a woman. Nothing less, nothing more.

Ruby was right, though. He was cute, and he was hers, for a little while at least.

"Yes, to both of those." Britney grinned.

"You really like him, don't you? I can see it in your eyes."

If Ruby could see it, Britney wondered if he could see it too. "I simply adore him." She gave a long sigh as she zeroed in on him. "I like his edges, his tattoos, the way his eyes light up when he excited. He's sweet and protective and loyal."

Gasping, Ruby touched her fingers to her mouth and smiled. "You've fallen for him."

"I tumbled right off the cliff," Britney said as she returned her gaze to Ruby. "Just, *whoosh*, and there I went."

"I'm happy for you."

Britney didn't know how to respond. Their relationship was fake. There was a host of obstacles between her heart and his. If they couldn't be tackled, they'd become barriers.

She mentally chided herself. Whatever happened, happened. She was glad she was spending time with him.

"Thank you, and thank you so much for inviting us

to spend the week here. It's been the best time." Britney grinned.

"I'd do anything for you." Ruby used her toes to play with the sand. "I don't know if I'd be here—"

"You stop that right now. You are beautiful, capable, and strong. You just needed a little support. That's all." Britney hugged her again. "You are one of the sweetest people I know, and I'm so happy for you and Doug. He's a lucky guy."

Just as Britney dropped her arms from Ruby, Hendrix rode a wave to the shore, picked up his board, and walked over. "Hey, I just want to say thanks for this. I've never been surfing before now, and it's a lot of fun."

Standing, Ruby smoothed her swimsuit cover-up and looked from Britney to Hendrix. "That makes me so, so happy to hear." She stepped closer, taking his arm and lifting on her toes. The crash of waves drowned out whatever Ruby was telling Hendrix. Britney wasn't sure how to feel about that.

He leaned back, a shocked expression on his face as stared at Ruby. She stepped back and nodded. Then he looked at Britney and said, "I'm not surprised by that at all."

Ruby pointed her finger at him. "My friend adores you, and if you hurt her, I will hunt you down and make you sorry." The sentence was spoken so quickly that it came out as one long word. She grinned and then shrugged, going from friendly to menacing and back in the span of a millisecond.

"No hunting needed. I'd wait for you because I'd deserve it."

A huge cheesy grin was followed by a giggle and a little shoulder shrug. "Obligatory threat checked off my list of friend duties, but I'm serious. Don't. See you guys at the luau." She bounced away toward her soon-to-be husband.

Hendrix shook his head, laughing. "She's a ball of energy, huh?" He stuck his board in the sand and sat next to Britney.

"She is, and I love her to pieces." Invisible ants were in her tankini bottoms, making her itch to know what Ruby said, but there was no way she was asking.

"You're just dying to know what she said to me."

"Am not."

Shaking his head, he nearly shook with laughter. "She said you were sweet, kind, gracious, and the best friend I could ever ask for."

"She didn't need to say that."

"She said you've been there for a lot of people. That you don't get near the attention you should."

Waving him off, she cleared her throat. "Ruby is my

closest friend. She's required by friendship law to say nice things."

With a lick of his lips, he grinned. "What's this adore stuff she was talking about?"

Rolling her eyes, Britney looked away. "The sun fried her brain."

Hendrix scooted a little closer. "She was sitting in the shade," he said, his voice dipping low. "You adore me, huh?"

Her mouth dropped open as she jerked her attention to him. "Don't you sexy-talk me. That's just not nice."

In the next second, he had her pulled over his lap, tickling her. "I'll show you nice."

She smacked his hands as she squealed, "Stop it."

"I like hearing you laugh."

"Then...tell...me...a...joke," she said between giggles.

Finally, he stopped, and she pointed her finger at him. "No more tickling."

"Fine. Killjoy." His gaze roamed over her face, an amused smile on his lips. "You are so beautiful, and it comes from such a deep place that time will never be able to take it from you."

Talk about a compliment. "No one has ever said anything like that to me before."

"Probably because they just assumed you knew. You can add humility to your list of character traits." He pressed his lips to her forehead, and when he leaned back, he sighed.

"Sweet talker." She grinned. "Did you want to surf some more?"

"Maybe a little longer, but I think I want a nap before the luau tonight."

"Oh yeah. I can't believe I almost forgot that's tonight." She hugged him around the neck. "Well, maybe we can stay until Sunday after the wedding and you can have a whole day. I don't know if it would be at the resort, but I'm sure we could find somewhere to stay."

It was a win-win for her. She didn't want her time with him to end. If he had fun surfing, it was all the better because she liked seeing him happy.

"All I heard was that I get to spend more time with you, and I'm good with that." He grinned, standing and pulling her to her feet.

"That sweet-talking is just digging the hole deeper, Mr. Wells." She pierced him with a look. "Just you wait."

He bent down, kissed her, and then darted away with his surfboard. "I look forward to it."

All she did was shake her head. That man. She took a deep breath and sat. She knew life with him wouldn't be cake and roses, but he was the kind of man to make promises and stand by them. That, more than anything, meant something to her. It meant that if she got sick, Hendrix would be there because he said he would be, and she could count on him.

Good looks, a great smile, and heaps of charm only lasted so long when the weather turned bad. It was how they manned the helm that counted. If nothing else, that's what her mom and dad's relationship had taught Britney. The situation was unique, but the lesson was still the same. Love was a commitment, and it wasn't for fair-weather partners.

That's what Britney wanted in a relationship. Solid ground when the whole world was shaking.

16

"What was it?" Hendrix answered his phone as he quickly stepped onto the back deck of the bungalow and shut the sliding glass door behind him. He didn't want Britney overhearing the conversation in case it was information that needed a delicate delivery. Noah had promised he'd call as soon as the lab results were back.

"Rohypnol. Just like you suspected."

Hendrix cursed under his breath and leaned his hip against the deck railing. "We have cameras everywhere, even the kitchen, and there was nothing."

"They were tampered with. Ryder and Mia are working on that now. Jax finally found the staff member, and he's working on getting their statement and corroborating it."

"Does Jax have the name of the suspect yet?"

The hesitation was too long on Noah's end.

"It's David Goss, isn't it?" Tension built in Hendrix's shoulders. He just didn't like that guy, and it had nothing to do with jealousy. "He was all over her."

Hendrix was positive David had deliberately spilled wine on himself so he could follow Britney. The matter of his hospital visit fueled that intense dislike too. David had called her shallow and made her cry. Hendrix had met his fair share of superficial people. He knew what they looked and sounded like. Britney didn't fit that definition by a long shot.

Not when she'd offered to stay an extra day just so he could surf a little more. It meant another day with her, and since her offer, Hendrix had spent a lot of his time trying to find reasons to add more days.

Noah snorted. "Yeah, but you need to keep it cool. That's why Jax is gathering the evidence to back up what the staff member relayed. The guy is old money, and he has a lot of it. Well, his dad anyway. David isn't far behind, though. His dad treated him much like my dad treated me. We worked for what we wanted. To be honest, this surprised me, and that doesn't happen often."

Hendrix was an idiot. It wasn't until then that he'd put billionaire and Britney in the same thought. Yeah, she'd taken him clothes shopping at an expensive store, but it hadn't hit home then at all. She was out of his league and out of his class. A billionaire. And Hendrix was...a novelty. That's why David had said it. An old-money billionaire and a guy like Hendrix were too far apart for him to even hope he could be the guy Britney needed.

The fact that she didn't act like she had that many zeros in her bank account didn't deduct from them. It meant she was kind and unaware of how the world worked because she hadn't lived in it like Hendrix. Getting involved with him would pull her into the uglier side of things. Man, he didn't want that. He wanted her glasses to be rose-colored. Her smile, her care, her essence. The world needed her as she was, not raw and weathered from dealing with him.

The dots were connecting in a way Hendrix hated. David wasn't the bad guy. He was the guy able to give Britney the life Hendrix couldn't.

"Noah, as much as I want it to be him, I don't think it is. I think the guy likes her and has liked her, and he thought this week would be a great way to reconnect with her. They seem to have a pretty good relationship." Hendrix pulled his hand from his pocket and raked it through his hair. "They had a verbal scuffle the day before she was released, but I think it's probably something they can get past."

Again, there was a lot of silence on Noah's end. It was the worst kind of silence too. Something heavy was about to drop from his boss's mouth, and Hendrix wasn't sure if he could handle it.

The silence continued to stretch, growing increasingly uncomfortable.

"What?" Hendrix asked.

"My little sister likes you. She has from the second she met you, and I saw the look in your eyes. The feeling was mutual. Sometimes it just happens. In the moment, you have no idea what's happening. You just know that your reality will never be the same again."

"Noah, if you knew..."

"What makes you think I don't?"

Hendrix's pulse jumped. "My records were sealed. That's how I know." The man he'd called Dad for two years made it happen, and that man didn't lie.

With a snort, Noah replied, "Haven't you noticed the hiring process for this company is unlike others? That I don't have the turnover that other companies have? Some have moved on to be with their families, but I don't have the hire/fire that's typical. I'm thorough, methodical, and, above all, informed."

"But..."

A soft laugh came from Noah. "There is nothing I don't know about you. I have two of the best computer people in the world working for me. I didn't hire you because you were perfect. I hired you because you made a choice to be a different man."

Hendrix walked to a nearby patio chair and dropped into it. "You mean..."

"I've known the whole time. Hendrix, when I hire people, I'm putting the lives of my team in their hands. We all have families and friends. I take our protection as seriously as I do our clients. I'm not bringing anyone on that I can't trust."

Mentally, Hendrix was using his arm to shield himself from the rocks hitting him. "I just always thought...I don't know. That you'd hired me because I was good at my job. I didn't have entanglements to get in the way."

"My relationship with Mia is *not* an entanglement." His tone held an edge. "Meeting her, trusting her... loving her has given me a freedom I never thought possible. She knows about all my darkness. I gave it to her. She wrapped her arms around it, and a weight was lifted from me. My past doesn't mean I can't love and be loved. No one on this earth loves Mia more than I do."

Hendrix hung his head. "You know Britney deserves better."

"That's the thing. Of course she does. Mia did too. But here I am, being loved by her, and she's given me a life that I'm grateful for. Would you believe she says the same about me? That I've seen her at her darkest and stood there without flinching?"

When Hendrix didn't respond right away, Noah said, "You've got choices to make, and you are the only one who can make them. Whatever you decide, you're still a member of my team. My family has never thrown people away. Never have, never will. You have a place here until you decide you don't want it."

"Thanks."

"All right, I'll be in touch if we find out anything more."

They ended the call, and Hendrix rubbed his hand over his hair. Noah had known his ugly details the whole time. From his homelife, to joining a gang, to running away and being found by an Alabama county sheriff. It was a heap to process. Any more punches to the head, and it would exceed his cognitive limits.

Just as the last thought floated through his head, he was attacked from the back, and stars exploded behind his eyes, the hit pitching him forward to the deck. He grabbed his head, and before he could catch up with what happened, something—someone—heavy was sitting on his chest, holding something over his nose and mouth.

His ears were still ringing, and now his lungs were protesting the lack of oxygen. After trying to throw the person off him, Hendrix managed to free one of his arms and swing it. For his effort, he got a grunt and what felt like a reaffirmation to smother him when the enemy punched him in the gut and then pressed down harder on his face.

Hendrix fought against letting himself float away, but the longer he went without air, the more his will crumbled. Just when he was about to let go, a shriek pierced the air. The pressure against his face lessened, and then the weight lifted.

"I'm calling an ambulance," Britney said in a rush.

"No," Hendrix strangled out. "I just need to catch my breath." He tried to push himself into a sitting position and failed. His next attempt was successful with Britney's help. "Did you see—" His voice caught as he coughed.

Britney replied, "No, I didn't see who it was." Her hands seemed to be everywhere as she tried to assess all that had happened. "You've got a nasty bump on your head."

He wanted to nod but knew it was a bad idea since

the headache throbbing behind his eyes would only get worse. "Yeah, I didn't see it coming."

"Can you stand?"

"Uh, I think so."

Just not on his own. It took Britney's help along with bracing himself against walls and furniture to get to his bedroom and lie down. He'd have stopped at the couch, but that thing was barely big enough for Britney.

"You need an ambulance."

Taking her hand, he whispered, "No, I'm okay. Just need some aspirin."

With a heavy sigh, she stood. "All right. I'll be just a second."

Time was relative. Whether it took a second or an hour, he had no idea. When she returned with water and medicine, he was grateful no matter how long it took.

The bed moved, and Britney hovered over him. "I texted Noah. I figured he needed to know." She bent a little lower. "Turn your head to the left a little for me. I think you're bleeding." She sucked air through her teeth. "Yeah, you are. Let me get something for that too."

When she returned, she had a towel and gently touched it to his head. "It's not a big cut, but you're going to feel it for a while." Then she lightly pressed a cold compress to the cut. "That should help too."

He held it to his head as he looked at her. "I'm okay. If not for you, I wouldn't have been." He chuckled and winced. "I just need to close my eyes for a bit. Then we can go to the luau."

A droplet of water hit his cheek, and he cracked his eyes open. Not water, tears, but with her head at the angle it was, she was trying to hide it. He tried to tip her chin up, and she fought him. "Britney, it's just a bump to the head. A gunshot is worse; I promise."

Her head jerked up, and those amazing blue eyes locked with his with tears pooling in them. "Shot?"

"I was in the Marines." It had happened once before that, but the answer he gave her was the safest until he had a head clear enough to actually have a conversation.

"That's not a good reason." Her bottom lip trembled, and she covered her mouth with her hand.

"Don't cry."

She ducked her head. "I'm not crying. It's hot in here...and I'm sweating through my eyes."

With a light tug, he wrapped his arm around her and pulled her to him. "I'm okay; I promise. If I wasn't, I'd tell you."

All he wanted was to soothe her. It broke his heart to know she was crying, and even more so knowing it was because of him. He pressed her closer and breathed her in. Maybe directing the conversation away from him would help. "I don't know what perfume that is, but I have never loved a scent more than I love this one." Man, he loved it.

"It's iris, jasmine, and sandalwood."

"That's why it fits you so well. Soft, sweet, and floral." He took in another long breath. "It's like they bottled your essence. Are you getting a cut?" He grunted a laugh.

"I know what you're doing. You're trying to change the topic, but you were almost killed, and it's my fault. You'll never be able to change that. I'm a horrible human being because I pulled you into this. I should've..." The sentence dissolved into sobs she tried to choke back.

He positioned his head in a way that the compress would stay put and wrapped his free arm around her. None of it was her fault, but he understood that guilt wasn't logical.

"You aren't horrible at all. Until we arrived on the island, they were harmless. You had no idea what would happen. Noah thinks they're close to finding them." He squeezed her a little closer. "We're going to catch them. Everything's going to be fine. I promise."

Hendrix believed every word he said, and he wasn't leaving until the jerk was caught.

17

Feeling wretched seemed to be Britney's way of life lately. "He was nearly killed, Noah."

"Nearly, but he's very much alive, and he'll be fine." Her brother was standing in the doorway to her bedroom, or that's what she suspected since she was sitting on her bed with her back to him. It had been nearly an hour since he and Ryder arrived. She and Noah had spoken briefly, and then he'd gone into detective mode with Ryder. What video footage they recorded hadn't helped because the attacker kept his head down.

Now, he was being a pest and wouldn't leave her alone. She hadn't been able to stop crying, and, oh, she hated it. It was okay for other people to cry, but for some reason, it wasn't okay for her.

Footsteps grew a little closer, and Britney eyed him

over her shoulder. “Don’t you dare. I’ll be fine. You need to keep a watch on Hendrix. A head injury of any type is dangerous, and since he refuses to go to the hospital, that’s our only option right now.” She pinched her lips together. Noah wouldn’t make him go either. Ticked her right off. Wasn’t that a boss’s job? To override their pigheaded employees?

“Hendrix is resting, and Ryder is keeping an eye on him while combing through footage. Jax would be here, but he’s tied up.” There was something Noah was leaving out, and normally Britney would have argued with him to spill it, but exhaustion was settling in.

Her shoulders sagged. “Noah, please leave me alone. I don’t want to talk anymore.”

He walked closer and sat on the end of the bed. “It’s *not* your fault. You had no idea it would lead to this, and you had no reason to think it would. You aren’t the only woman in the world this has happened to. I tell them the same thing I’m telling you.”

“But, Noah—”

“No. I don’t care. This is not your fault. You are the victim in this, and Hendrix is doing his job. He knew the risk when he agreed to accompany you to this wedding.” Noah stretched his hand out and touched her shoulder. “This isn’t the first stalker he’s dealt with.”

“You should listen to him,” Hendrix said.

Britney jumped and angled further away. "You're supposed to be resting. Go lie down. You have a head injury."

"Headache's gone, it's a barely-there cut, and I'm fine." Hendrix chuckled. "We have a luau to attend."

"I'm not going. Your headache would probably come back, so you don't need to go either." She snatched a tissue from the box sitting next to her and wiped her nose. "Now, both of you go."

Noah stood and walked to the door. "It's not your fault. Stop blaming yourself. If this were anyone else, you'd be telling them the same thing, and you know it."

Maybe she would, but that was her role in the world, right? To be there when people needed it? It was about all she was good for. There was a chance she was being overly hard on herself, but her heart hurt.

When the door clicked shut, she collapsed forward and bawled. She was the one who'd seen it happen. Seeing violence in person wasn't anything like seeing it in the movies or news articles or videos. It was shocking, and the scene was branded in her mind. She couldn't stop the vision of Hendrix fighting for his life. It was... every ugly word known to man all mixed together.

"Your brother is right," Hendrix said softly.

Britney startled and bolted straight up. "I thought I told you to go lie down, hardheaded man. Now, get."

With a chuckle, he said, "Come make me."

Rotten man too. She didn't want him to see her cry again. Knowing he was hearing it was bad enough. "That's a dirty trick, Mr. Wells."

She looked up, pleading to whoever might be watching that her tears would stop. No one heard her, though, because they only seemed to fall faster.

"What has you so upset? It can't just be me."

"Why not? You have immeasurable value to me." She swallowed hard. "Noah runs a company that protects people. Zach flies medical equipment to Jamaica. Julian paints and teaches free children's art classes. And Zoe founded a non-profit that provides free medical and dental care to those who can't afford it." Her siblings did these grand things, and she was so proud of them. Britney understood it wasn't a competition, but that didn't change the need to feel useful.

"What do I do? Pretend like a stalker is somehow funny and nothing to be concerned about. I plan parties. Nothing of any value." She took a deep shuddering breath. "You say I deserve better...but...with how I treated this whole situation—you—that can't possibly be true. At least whatever you did is in the past. My failures...are right in front of me."

A second later, Hendrix was next to her and pulling her into an embrace with her back against his chest and his chin on her shoulder. "No, Britney. You're kind and caring, more than you give yourself credit for. And according to Ruby, you've been a light to many who needed sunshine in their lives."

"I sure don't feel that way." She stretched and grabbed the tissue box, snatching another tissue out. "Those things were little. Being a friend? That's easy."

"Not for everyone. Definitely not for me. I couldn't have done that. Ruby was suicidal. Her soon-to-be husband is marrying a wonderful woman because you loved her. And I know she's wonderful because she's friends with you."

Britney dabbed her eyes with the tissue. Ruby shouldn't have told him that. "She's making it out to be more than it was."

"No, she isn't." He took a deep breath and slowly let it out. "You're a lockbox for secrets, right?"

"Yes, I am." At least that was one thing she did right. Secrets came to her and they went nowhere else.

"Will you let me be yours?"

Groaning, she pressed the side of her head against his cheek. "Stop being sweet to me. I'm trying to stop crying."

"Look, this will sound hypocritical, but I promise I'm working on it." His grip loosened on her, and he took one hand away to brush her hair to the side and touched his lips to her neck. "If we're friends, it can't be one-sided."

"Why are you being logical at a time like this? I need to feel miserable." She couldn't even argue with him. He was only asking for the same trust she was.

"Talk to me," he whispered.

When she didn't respond, he pressed his lips to her neck a little lower and held them there a second. "Come on."

Her heart, mind, and body seemed to find the same page, and she wilted against him. She needed to put up or shut up. A relationship—even a simple friendship—was a two-way street. If he was going to confide in her, didn't she need to trust him too?

"I've never seen anything like that before. You were fighting for your life, and I didn't want to lose you. It scared me, and I'm the reason for it. I care about you, Hendrix, and it's almost like you don't value your own life. But...I do. Your stay on this earth is of great importance to me. The longer the better." The words rushed out at tongue-breaking speed, but having them out did seem to alleviate some of the ache in her heart.

He was quiet for a moment, and she could feel his smile against her skin. "You have my promise that from this point forward, I will put my safety at the forefront of my mind in anything I do. My desire to stay on this earth has grown considerably since this past Friday." As he spoke, his breath tickled her skin. It was innocent and intimate and nerve-wracking all at once.

She couldn't stop herself from smiling. "Are you telling the truth about how you're feeling? That you don't have a headache and the cut is small?"

"I promise I am."

"I do have a dress I was saving for the luau, and I still have plenty of time to get ready. I guess if you're feeling okay, we can go."

The chest-deep rumble of his laughter carried through her body. "I'd very much like to see you in the dress you saved for tonight."

"With sandals."

"You have very cute toes."

"With my hair down."

He moaned against her shoulder. "I think this should classify as torture."

She rolled her lips in, working to stifle a chuckle. "Okay, I'll get ready, but I don't want you to see me red-nosed with my eyes all puffy again."

"All right, but this is the last time I agree to that. If you're going to see me at my worst, it's only fair I see you at yours," he said as he released her and stood. "And I mean that."

He made a good point. She couldn't expect him to

trust her if she didn't trust him. "But are you going to let me see you at your worst?"

"I'm in the process of working up my courage, but as it stands, you're the only person on this earth I trust whole-heartedly. This is a situation of 'It's not you; it's me.'" He sighed. "I haven't really trusted anyone in a long time, and...I'm scared."

"Okay. You have a deal." She went to turn but stopped and hesitated a second before facing him. "I'll go first."

Their eyes locked, and she could see the concern in his. "You haven't been sleeping well. How have I not noticed that?" he asked.

A tiny smile lifted her lips. "It seems I owe a five-star review to the company that produces my concealer."

"Seems so," he said. "We rectify that tonight, okay?"

"Only if it's mutual."

His lips quirked into one of his knee-weakening brilliant smiles. "All right." With a wink, he opened the door and shut it behind him.

In the stillness of the room, she pressed the flat of her hand over her heart. She was in love with Hendrix, and the word didn't even alarm her. On the island. Off the island. Friends or not. Every beat of her heart belonged to him. No matter how their lives moved forward from this point, she loved him.

She'd leave it unspoken for the time being, but not because of fear. When she said it, she didn't want him feeling pressured to say it in return. She wanted his love willingly when he was ready. Until then, she'd relish the shoulder he'd offered and be the friend he needed her to be.

Now it was time to get ready and show him what real torture looked like.

18

In the quiet of his room, Hendrix propped his feet on the desk in front of the wall of monitors. Noah and Ryder had left a while ago, and since then, Hendrix had nothing to do but think—and all of it centered around Britney.

Noah had stepped out of his room, and she'd gone to pieces. Worse than she had after the stuffed pig or the hospital stay. Both heartbreaking and sweet at the same time. She'd lost sleep over him and wept for him. His life was valuable to her. The only other person who'd shown him that sort of consideration was the small-town country sheriff who'd taken him in when he was fourteen.

His phone rang, and he answered it. "Hey." He was a little surprised Noah was calling so quickly.

"We know who it is. It's just a matter of getting everything together. It's David Goss, but you can't tell Britney until we have him in custody. She'll never believe it, and we have definitive proof that it's him. If you tell her, she'll call him, and with his money, he could disappear and we'd never find him."

The information should have been comforting, but Hendrix found himself anything but. "Really? I just don't think so."

"You were sure just a couple of days ago."

"Yeah, I was, but when I looked at things from his perspective, it changed my opinion." But if it wasn't David, who was it? "You said you have proof?"

"Yes, and it's as solid as we could have hoped for. He won't be getting out of it."

Hendrix couldn't argue with that. "All right. I just don't know if I'm comfortable keeping it from her. She won't be happy about that."

Noah laughed. "I know. I'll take the blame."

"Just know I won't do it again."

"I guess you've made a choice?"

"I've made the choice that I won't push her further away. That means no more secrets other than the ones I'm already chewing on." Over the last couple of days, any time Hendrix was alone, he was deep in thought when it came to her. One such thought was telling her about his past.

When she'd faced him, he'd been shocked at how ragged she looked. She was still beautiful; that didn't change. But she'd let him *see* her. The vulnerable side she locked away from the rest of the world. Hers looked way different than his, but he knew what anguish looked like. In that respect, they were a matching pair.

Shaken by the attack, she'd lost sleep and wept over him. His life had worth, and she grieved at the thought she could lose him. *Him.* She cared about him, and when combined with the conversation he'd had with Noah, it was rather life-changing. Noah knew him...and still put his sister's life in Hendrix's hands.

Even more amazing, he was being entrusted with her heart as well. It was a heavy, thought-provoking responsibility.

"Good choice." Noah went silent a second. "Last piece of advice."

Last? Hendrix hoped not. "Okay."

"Don't wait to tell her you love her. Our jobs don't give us the luxury of thinking we'll always come home. If something happens to me, I know Mia will have no room for doubt that I love her. I say it to the point of nausea sometimes, but I'd rather say it too much than not often enough."

Love. That was a big word, but he was closer to saying it than he'd ever been before, and he couldn't see ever wanting to say it to anyone other than Britney. "I'll keep that in mind."

"Hendrix?" Britney called his name.

With the phone still to his ear, he stood, crossed the room to the door, and opened it. "I have...to let you go." He didn't wait for a response before ending the call and slipping the phone into his pocket.

Even with the description she'd given him earlier, he was ill-prepared for the perfection standing across the living room. "Britney..." Every word that came to mind lacked sufficient definition for her.

Her long dark hair was swept to one side and fastened at the nape of her neck with a waterfall of waves flowing halfway down her arm. The teal color of the dress complimented the color of her eyes while making her skin look soft and warm. If that weren't enough, it stopped at her knees, showing off her incredible legs. Then those adorable little toes peeked from her sandals.

There was so much more to her than just her appearance, creating the insatiable hunger to wrap his arms around her and forget about the luau. He adored her and the remarkable inner beauty that made her glow.

He strode across the room and stopped in front of her. "I just don't have words."

A blanket of pink covered her cheeks. Blushing? It was obvious she'd been complimented before, but the fact that she showed a physical reaction made her even more tantalizing.

"I wanted to look nice for you." She lifted her gaze to his. "As long as you like it, I don't care about anyone else."

"I...I definitely like it." Brushing a piece of hair from her face, he bent down and kissed her. "I'm struggling to accept how fortunate I am that I met you."

She sighed. "And you're just a girl's dream come true. All handsome and sexy." She took a half-step closer. "You have a host of character traits that lead me to believe I'm the lucky one."

Hendrix stared at her, slack-jawed. "How do you do that?"

"Do what?"

"I tell you that I'm not someone worth knowing, and you don't back away. That I have nothing but darkness to offer. You just...smile and pour all your sunshine into someone. Me. It's like you have no fear."

Palming the spot over his heart, she said, "If that's the case, you're the one who's fearless because darkness cowers when it's flooded with light, yet here you are, standing right in front of me." She moved her hand to his face. "I see your light, Hendrix. I feel it when you wrap your arms around me."

His eyebrows knitted together. "How so?"

"You hold me like I'm cherished. It makes me feel special. Like…I finally found my place in the world."

"I could say the same of you," he said softly.

Wrapping his arms around her, he brushed his lips across hers and then trailed them along her jaw, skimming her addictively sweet skin. With a gasp, she balled her hands in his shirt and pressed her body against his as her head tipped back.

He continued the tease, moving from her jaw to her neck before returning to her lips and hovering just a breath away, letting their breath mingle.

Her eyes opened, immediately locking with his. He'd never had need mirrored back at him.

"*Kiss me*," she pleaded.

He studied her face, memorizing the lines and curves. The way her expressive blue eyes seemed to beg him to kiss her in ways her mouth couldn't articulate.

Taking one arm from her waist, he brought his hand to her mouth and rubbed his thumb over her soft, supple lips, pausing at the corner.

Without breaking eye contact, she parted her lips and wrapped them around his thumb, gently kissing it.

Her fists tightened in his shirt, trying to bring his mouth closer to hers. "Please, kiss me."

The second the command was off her tongue, his will to lengthen the moment collapsed. Not a breath later, his mouth was on hers, coaxing her lips to part, desperate to taste her. Her warm body melted into his with a sharp gasp, followed by a moan as their mouths moved together in an unhurried, languid dance.

Flattening his hand against her back, he erased what little space was left between them. He wanted her. To intertwine his soul against hers until it was indistinguishable. In that moment, he realized it didn't matter what became of this, his heart was hopelessly and eternally hers.

When his lungs cried for air, he reluctantly broke the kiss. "We should probably go to the luau."

Britney gulped air. "Probably." She set her forehead against his chin as her chest rose and fell against his. "I never understood the term *drunk on someone* until now, and I don't ever want to be sober again."

Leaning back, he was stunned into silence. He'd already thought she was beautiful. Flushed face, swollen lips, and passion-hazed eyes took her to a level of sexy he'd never seen before. More so, knowing he was the cause.

"I might have to agree," he said and smiled.

Their embrace lasted just a breath longer, and they released each other.

"One second. I need to check my makeup." She touched her fingers to her lips.

She still looked perfect to him. "You don't need to."

As she walked to her room, she said, "Charmer."

He took the moment to straighten his shirt before she returned, looking much the same to him. He was smart enough to keep that to himself, though. They linked their fingers and walked to the door.

After setting the bungalow alarm, they reached the steps, and she stopped him on the next-to-last step. Taking his face in her hands, she kissed him, circled her arms around his neck, and said, "If you think I won't be repaying that delightfully torturous kiss with one as equally so...or more..." She paused, taking his earlobe between her teeth and running her tongue along the edge. "You would be wrong." She leaned back, winked, and pranced away.

It was like she was given a map of all the things that drove him crazy. He shook his head and cleared his thoughts before jogging to catch up with her. "You are..."

The hitch of her eyebrow made him pause. Did he really want to antagonize her after what she'd just threatened? The sad reality was that part of him was screaming *yes*.

He was with it enough to finish with, "...gorgeous tonight."

"Thank you." But she said it like she knew that wasn't what he'd planned to say. She sighed, wrapping her arms around his bicep. "It's so pretty out here tonight. No clouds, and stars seemingly infinite."

"Yeah, it is." What fell out of his mouth next was a clear indication that his brain was in kamikaze mode. "With the breeze, it's a good night for a walk on the beach."

She gasped. "That's a lovely idea."

"I wasn't suggesting we should. I just...you know... was pointing it out."

"Is there a problem, Mr. Wells? Do you foresee trouble should we enjoy a moonlit walk under the stars?" It was that same *gotcha* tone she'd had in the burger restaurant.

In one swift move, he spun around, picked her up, and kissed her nose. "You aren't nearly as funny as you think you are."

Her head fell back as she squealed with laughter. When she returned her gaze to him, the levity was gone. She set her fingertips against his forehead then drew them down the side of his face until they met at his chin.

"Oh, what you do to my heart, Mr. Wells." She pressed a light kiss to his lips. "I'm finding myself in a predicament."

His tongue was frozen a second. "What sort of predicament?"

"I asked you to be mine for the week, and as the minutes pass, the more I belong to you and I hope it never ends."

The air in his lungs vanished. The confession both terrified him and gave him life. "It seems our fates are intertwined at this juncture." Just a week ago, it would have felt like a bear trap. Now, being entangled with her felt less like a prison and more like unbelievable freedom. To love and be loved.

"Is that so?"

"Maybe the walk on the beach will come with ghost stories." He was going to tell her everything. The risk was inconsequential now that his heart was hers. It was simply a step forward...with her.

She laid her hands on his chest, fanning her fingers out, and ran them over his shoulders and down his arms. "I'm sure with all your muscles and experience, I'll be absolutely safe. Fearless even."

"I doubt you need me for that."

Tilting her head, she replied, "Need? Maybe not.

Want? Absolutely. There's strength in numbers, Hendrix."

"Yeah," he said, returning her feet to the walkway. What he didn't say was that he felt like Hercules when she was next to him. "Let's get to the luau. I bet the show is about to start, if we haven't already missed it."

With a slight pause, she nodded as they wound their way through the resort to the beach near the restaurant. Ruby was speaking, and she blew a kiss in Britney's direction as they found their seats.

David, sitting across the way and a few seats down, smiled at Britney. She returned it and waved. "He's not a bad guy. I think he thought I was familiar, and he was lonely. I'm guessing he thought we'd reconnect here." She looked at Hendrix. "It wouldn't have happened. I never had any such feelings for him. We're friends, and that's it."

Hendrix watched the guy a second, wondering if his boss would be showing up to crash the luau. His phone buzzed in his pocket, and he discreetly pulled it out, checking the screen.

We know he's at the luau. As soon as it ends, police will move in, the text from Noah said.

"Something wrong?" Britney asked.

Hendrix pushed the phone back in. "No, just thinking that's the conclusion I've come to."

She shot him a coy smile. "Not jealous anymore."

Shaking his head, Hendrix replied, "No." He felt sorry for him. One, that David had missed his chance with Britney—though Hendrix was not sorry enough to step out of the way for him to have another chance. And two, the guy was facing a prison sentence for stalking. Either way, the universe had smiled down on Hendrix, and he wasn't taking it for granted.

With a bump of her shoulder against his, she grinned. "Good. Not sure what changed, but I'm glad you aren't."

Hendrix leaned over and set his cheek against hers. "You don't look at him the way you look at me."

Her hand came to rest on the side of his face, pressing his cheek tighter against hers. "No, I don't. You hold my heart in your hands."

Pulling back, he caught her gaze. What should he say to that? What *could* he say to that? No one had ever trusted him like that before. Granted, he'd never wanted the responsibility before now. He'd actively run from it. He wasn't going to run from her, though. Not when it seemed she needed him as much as he needed her.

Just as he went to respond, drums sounded, and the show began. Probably for the best. A luau wasn't where he wanted this conversation to begin. Once he started, he didn't want to stop until it was all out.

There was still a little hesitation. To deny it would be lying, but he trusted her more than he feared rejection. A weird, new sensation. One he could see himself enjoying.

19

At some point during the show, Britney had moved into Hendrix's lap with her back against his chest and his arms wrapped around her, like he was keeping her from slipping away. If there was a heaven, this was hers.

Every time she rested her head on his shoulder, she inhaled the scent of his soap mixed with salty air and melted further into him. He was a hot bath after a long day. The person created for her, fitting like he was custom-made. It gave her an incredible sense of peace.

Then there was that kiss.

That kiss.

Heady, mind-blowing, sensual, and soul-shaking. With his lips hovering just out of reach, it was agony. He'd held her gaze, and unlike the men she'd dated in the past, she didn't see lust in his eyes. She saw adoration, savoring. He wasn't just touching his lips to hers; he was drinking her in and loving her in ways that words couldn't convey.

The only downside was the luau. As soon as the opportunity presented itself, she was going to show him just how soul-bound to him she was. She loved him, and there wasn't a story he could tell that would change that fact.

He set his lips against her ear. "I don't think I could twirl fire like those guys. I'd burn the island down."

"No." She giggled as his breath tickled her skin.

She tilted her head a little to the side, and he pressed a kiss to her neck. "I'm finding it increasingly difficult to refrain from kissing you."

The warmth of his breath rolled down her spine, and she shivered. He brushed aside the pieces of hair that had fallen from the hair tie, pressed his lips to her bare shoulder, and trailed feathery kisses to the other. Her eyes slid closed, and all she wanted to do was to sink into him.

When his mouth returned to her neck, he moaned, and the chest-deep rumble sent a tremor through her. "I think I could sit just like this forever and never get bored."

Lifting her shoulder, she smiled. "I certainly wouldn't mind."

After their meal, she and Hendrix wound their way through the people to Ruby, and Britney hugged her. "This was fantastic."

"This was the only way to show how much I appreciate the people in my life, especially you." Ruby held her at arm's length. "You look so pretty tonight."

"You look fabulous. Aquamarine is your color."

They embraced again, and Ruby squeezed her. "Two weeks. Pedicures. And a whole dish waiting to be filled with all the Hendrix details you want to divulge." Ruby glanced at Hendrix and winked.

"There isn't a bowl big enough for that." Britney grinned when his cheeks flushed.

He ducked his head as he shook it. The quirk on his lips betrayed him, though. As much as he protested it, his body language spoke something completely different.

Another couple approached, and Britney wrapped her arms around Hendrix's bicep. "We'll see you tomorrow."

"See you tomorrow."

On the walk to the bungalow, Britney laid her head on his arm, enjoying the rustle of the warm breeze through the vegetation and the distant sound of the crashing waves. "I love this island."

"Me too, but it might be for different reasons."

She lifted her gaze to his. "Maybe, but I don't think so." She'd had a magical evening with Hendrix. Kissing him. Being kissed by him. The velvety texture of his lips gliding across her skin.

Hendrix pulled her to a stop. He set his hands on her shoulders and slid them down her arms. Taking her hands, he placed them around his neck and then slid his hands along her back until he was curled around her.

A slight bend, and he was kissing her. On her toes, she angled herself so there was nothing between her body and his. A growl ripped from his throat as he lifted her and crushed his lips against hers.

Unlike the previous kiss, this one was hot and hard and heady. A frenzy of tangled mouths and whimpers of a want so deep and wide she felt flayed open. The fever of the moment slowly cooled until her head was tilted back and feathery kisses were pulling her down into madness.

Just as she dipped her toe in, his hand cupped the back of her head and his lips returned to hers. "I was wrong when I said might. I completely agree—I never want to be sober again. A thousand times a day for a thousand years will never satisfy me."

"Endlessly so," she whispered. "As much as I enjoy this, I'm in the mood for a few ghost stories. If…you…"

"Yeah, I do." He gently pressed a kiss to her forehead, and the warm breeze turned cool as they began walking again.

When they reached the bungalow, Noah was waiting on the porch. "You're not going to like this," he said to Britney.

She followed him with Hendrix trailing behind her. She stepped inside, and her breath caught. "David?"

Tied to a chair, he strained against it. "It's not me. I got a text from you to meet you here. I thought you'd left the luau early too. I was doing what you asked."

"A text? But I didn't." She took her phone from her clutch, checking it. "See?" She held it up to him. "Nothing."

"It'll be way easier on you if you just admit you've been stalking her." Noah set his hands on his hips. He looked at Britney. "There was no text on his phone either."

"What?" David glared at Noah. "It was there. Why would I stalk Britney? I've known her forever. There's no logic to this at all."

Hendrix took a half-step closer. "Did you find him inside?"

"Yeah, wires to the security systems were cut." Noah

tipped his head to Hendrix's room. "We got him on video, though."

"What wires? Video? Can someone just explain to me what's going on? I don't even understand what I'm being accused of doing." David looked from Noah to Britney. "I was a jerk the other day, but I'm not a *stalker*. The text said you were making coffee and to just come on in. That you wanted to talk about the other day." He shrugged. "I thought it was weird because the luau was tonight, but I just assumed that you'd left early."

Hendrix crossed his arms over his chest. "He didn't do this. Something's not right about it."

"Wait." David blinked. "You believe me?"

Nodding, Hendrix said, "Yeah. I do."

Noah beckoned them with his finger to follow him to Hendrix's bedroom. "Ryder, show them what you have."

Britney dropped her clutch on the end table as she went to the room and stopped in front of the monitor clearly showing David cutting the security wires and then breaking into the bungalow.

"What David didn't know was that we had a backup system. When he cut the wires, it tripped that. A silent alarm was sent to my phone, and from there I called the police. That is David Goss. There is no denying it."

Image after image appeared on the screen. Pictures

of David. Receipts showing a drone purchase. Stuffed animals. How could she refute what Noah was presenting?

"Yeah..." Hendrix's eyebrows knitted together, and he rubbed his knuckles along his jaw. "Really can't argue against all that."

"You don't seem as surprised as me. Did you know it was him?" Britney asked.

Noah held up a finger. "He did, and I'll take the blame for keeping it from you. I told him not to tell you. I didn't want you confronting David and ruining our chance of catching him."

"I'm sorry," Hendrix said.

"It's okay. Unfortunately, Noah's right. I would have." Looking over her shoulder, Britney pinched her lips together. "I've known David a long time, and I'm struggling to believe this, even with it staring me in the face. I wasn't even aware he was this knowledgeable about security systems or other tech things."

"He probably did like most people and hunted down the information on the internet." Noah's posture softened. "I know it's hard. You think you know someone, and reconciling what you know with the truth shakes your faith in yourself a little. It happens a lot."

"I guess it's over, then?" Even as she said it, it didn't quite reach her heart. She crossed the room back to

David. "They have you on film, and there's no text on my phone or yours."

David groaned. "It's not me. I swear."

How was it that, logically, she could see his guilt but not feel it? It didn't make sense. *It was right there.* "This sounds awful, but I don't know what to believe."

"I know, and I have no way to prove it's not me." He grumbled under his breath. "Britney, I was alone when I got your text. I'm not a member of the wedding party, so I haven't been going to the events. That first night, Ruby was generous enough to let me crash it, but that was it until yesterday when she and I ran into each other. She said I could come to the luau tonight, and I didn't even stay. I saw you with Hendrix and left right after. Most of my time has been spent alone."

"The drone?" she asked, trying to find a way to poke holes in his guilt.

He shrugged. "Just thought it was cool."

"And the stuffed animals?"

Shaking his head, he replied, "They're on my credit card, but I didn't buy them."

"The drug in my food? Attacking Hendrix?"

David's eyebrows knitted together. "Attack? Drug? What attack and what drug?" He looked in Hendrix's direction. "As for him? We talked about that. I may not be the sexiest man in the world, but I like my face the way it is." With a sigh, he hung his head. "And you know me well enough that you have to believe I would have never done that."

She would have...before...

A knock came from the door, and two uniformed officers stood there. In minutes, they were handcuffing David and walking him out the door. Part of Britney wanted to step in front of them and plead his innocence, while the other part felt relief that she didn't have to worry about Hendrix anymore.

Ryder joined them in the living room. "I guess there's no need for a security system anymore." He directed the statement to Noah.

"That depends. Hendrix?"

"I don't know. It's pretty clear he was the one stalking you." Hendrix crossed the room and stopped in front of Britney. "Would you feel better if the system were restored?"

Would she? The stalker was caught, and based on what her brother said, it was normal to feel out of sorts. Her feelings didn't change what was on the screen. "I think it'll be okay." She lifted her gaze to Hendrix. "I mean, we saw him, right?"

"We did." He put his arm around her. "But this isn't about him. This is about you. What do you want?"

"I want it on."

Noah cleared his throat. "Okay, we'll get it up and running."

Hendrix nodded toward Noah. "Are you okay if I help them?"

"Sure. I'm going to wash my face." She put her mouth to his ear. "Maybe instead of a walk, we can just camp under the stars."

"Okay." He kissed her forehead and turned to Ryder. "Well, let's get to work."

Britney slipped inside her bedroom, shut the door, and walked to the bathroom. She wasn't sure if she was stunned or relieved. She'd known David long enough that she would never have believed him capable had it not been for the security footage. While she was glad the stalker was caught, it did make her question herself. How had she not seen it? Even after he'd accused her of being shallow, it had never crossed her mind.

Bracing her hands against the sink counter, she leaned forward and hung her head. At least it was over, and she could move on. Besides, she was eager to learn more about Hendrix and his so-called ghost stories.

Not thirty minutes later, Hendrix dropped onto the blanket Britney had spread out just a few feet from the back deck, far enough from the deck that she was pretty sure the security system wouldn't be privy to any of his secrets. "Hi. At least it didn't take too long."

She covered her mouth as she yawned. “It gave me time to wash my face, brush my hair, and put pajamas on.” Exhaustion did come close to how tired she was, but she was determined to stay awake.

She leaned her head against his shoulder. “Thank you for fixing the security. I know David is caught, but...”

“You have a right to feel confused. I was having a hard time believing it, and I just met the guy.”

“I just...how did I not know? Even you said the timing fit.”

“Most people don’t know it’s someone close to them. That’s why it goes on for so long. We see these people every day, and it’s easy to feel betrayed, by them and ourselves.”

Lying back, he sighed. “I was tired, and now I’m wiped out.”

She lay next to him, stretched her arm across his chest, and groaned. “That was a terrible mistake.” She went to sit up, and he stopped her. “I don’t want to fall asleep on you.”

Both of his arms circled around her. “It was a long week. You’ve been worried and stressed. An ordeal like this is hard on a person mentally.”

“But you were going to tell me ghost stories. I feel terrible because I want to hear them.”

With a kiss, he said, "You have my promise that I will tell you. For now, let's enjoy the night and rest."

Britney relaxed again. "Ruby would be upset if I were a zombie tomorrow for dance lessons and then the rehearsal. I have to pick up my mom too, and then there's the bachelorette party. Good thing I planned that plenty in advance. It would have been a mess if I hadn't."

"See? All the more reason to get some sleep."

"Compromise?"

"Like what?" He rolled his head to look at her.

She chewed her lip. "Just one story. A small one. The beginning maybe?"

"Okay, just one." He paused. "My biological dad was abusive. I don't have a single memory of him where he wasn't beating on my mom. When we were really small, my granny—on my dad's side—would pick up me and Walker. We lived in the country in Arkansas a few miles from town. As we got older, she'd send us to the neighbors a field away."

That was awful at any age, but a child? Her heart broke for him. She squeezed his chest, hoping he felt her support to keep going.

"At some point, I guess we got old enough that we didn't need sheltering anymore. Either that or my mom was so tired she just didn't care. He'd beat us. I'd go to school with marks all over me, but it didn't matter. Small town, everyone knew everyone, and no one wanted to butt in, I guess."

Tears pooled in her eyes. She couldn't imagine such a thing. "No one ever said anything?"

"My granny tried a little, but she kept thinking he'd get right with God and stop. She died when I was about seven, and from there it got worse." He yawned. "I think I'll stop there."

What? She lifted up on her elbow. "That's some cliffhanger."

"It's hard to talk about, and when I'm tired, it gets to me more."

She brushed his hair back and then combed her fingers through it. "Actually, that makes a lot of sense. When you're tired, everything is amplified."

He knitted his eyebrows together. "You aren't going to push me?"

Shaking her head, she replied, "I'm only listening because you want to tell me. It won't change a thing."

I promise. She'd memorized where his tattoo was and began tracing it with her finger. "I promise I will never let anyone hurt you again. I don't care what mountains I need to move, glass I need to crawl through, or bodies I need to step over—I will make good on that promise." She tapped the tattoo. "I mean that."

"I believe you," he said softly.

She rested her head on his shoulder, laying her arm across his chest and snuggling closer.

Stories or no stories, she loved him. She knew it was important to him that he tell her, though. That he needed time to trust her. She'd take his tattered heart that people had left in their wake and gently sew him back together. It was a choice she planned to make for as long as she lived.

20

After nearly breaking Britney's toes and then picking her mom up from the airport, Hendrix had returned them to the resort. From the moment he woke up, he'd been going back and forth about David.

Something wasn't right. It made zero sense, but to his way of thinking, it was better to ask questions now than live with the niggling thought that he'd sent an innocent man to jail.

"Hey," Noah said as he opened his hotel room door. Noah had booked a suite for the small team a little over a mile from the resort. "What's up? I thought you were having lunch with Britney and my mom. I was just about to leave to meet up with you guys." He moved aside to allow Hendrix entry.

"I was, but I want to look over the evidence again." He stopped and turned to Noah as he shut the door. "It's still bothering me."

Rufus trotted into the room and gave a soft bark, like, *Oh, it's just you*, and then went back into the room he'd come from.

Noah walked past him to a table in the corner near a moderate-size kitchenette. "Okay, but what's bothering you? I mean, we've got him."

"I know, and I don't have a clear reason why."

"Have you told Britney this?"

Hendrix shook his head and joined Noah at the table. "No. I wanted to go over everything again before mentioning it. If I'm wrong, then she'll be worrying again for nothing."

"Good call." Noah booted up the laptop and pulled up the file folder holding all the information they had. "Where do you want to start? The beginning?"

"No, let's start with last night. When he cut the system wires."

Ryder walked into the shared living space and stopped. "Hey, what's up? I thought the two of you would be enjoying lunch by now."

"Hendrix wants to go over what we have again." Noah looked over his shoulder.

"Three sets of eyes are better than two," Ryder replied, crossing the room and stopping behind Noah.

Jax stepped out of his room holding a t-shirt. "Need a fourth?"

"Sure," Hendrix replied.

Noah hit play on the video, and they watched a couple of times before Hendrix said, "Pause it."

"I don't see anything different than what I saw last night," Noah said.

Hendrix studied the image a second. "Is it just me, or is the guy looking straight into the camera?"

"A little." Jax nodded.

Ryder shrugged. "Sort of, but it could just be the angle of the camera. I mean, I did put it in a position to get the best possible face shot."

Again, Hendrix couldn't argue. "Yeah."

Pushing out of the chair, Noah looked at Hendrix. "Like I said, you're free to go over it. I just don't see how you're going to come to a different conclusion. This is as clear-cut as it gets."

"I still want to go through it, but you go ahead and meet up with your mom and sister. I don't know how long I'll be." Hendrix took the laptop and set it in front of him. "I'll be back in plenty of time to get ready for the rehearsal."

Noah cocked his head. "Are you in the wedding?"

"No, I'll be in the audience. We've got an after-rehearsal dinner to attend."

"Okay. Well, I'm off to enjoy a tongue-lashing from my mother for making her stay in Houston after Britney was put in the hospital." He groaned and walked to the door. "If you three see something, let me know. Like, really, make it urgent. And as soon as possible."

Hendrix snorted as Noah walked out the door and, chuckling, turned his attention back to the screen. He sighed. "What am I missing? I mean, he's right there, and I'm questioning it. It doesn't make any sense."

Ryder took the seat Noah had just vacated and shrugged. "I don't know."

Hendrix looked at Jax. "I mean, I wanted it to be him. It's basically a wish come true, and here I am, trying to spring the guy." Hendrix crossed his arms over his chest, directing the next set of questions to Ryder. "Did you call the credit card company and check the stuffed-animal purchases? Where they might have come from?"

"Yeah, the statement had a number on it." Ryder pulled the laptop over a little and typed in a web address. "That's it. Ralph's Magic and More. The owner's name is Rick. Weird, but apparently he purchased it from the original owner. It's a cool little store, but when I called, they said they didn't keep receipts beyond seven days, which is the number of days in the refund policy."

Hendrix scooted his chair over a little and began flipping through the photos. There weren't a ton, but it gave a good idea of what they carried. Collectibles like comics, figurines, and cosplay-type items. "Interesting place. Check out those masks."

"I hadn't seen those." Jax braced his hand on the back of Ryder's chair and leaned in. "Those look like movie-prop quality. That's some serious detail."

Ryder nodded. "Yeah, I know. When I called, I asked about them, and the woman on the phone said the owner gets them in every so often. She doesn't know where he gets them, though, because the guy doesn't want to give out his source. I can see his point. Those alone probably account for half the profits."

"I guess that's a bust." Hendrix closed the page. "How about the drone?"

Ryder shrugged. "It is the same brand as the one we found back home in the dumpster, but it's really popular, so that's not a nail in the coffin."

Hendrix twisted in the seat and looked at Jax. "What about the resort employee? Anything there seem off to you?"

Shaking his head, Jax replied, "Not really. I mean, it was hard to track him down, but the excuse was valid.

He works two jobs, and one of them is taking tourists on long trails and camping out. He'd just returned from one." He shrugged. "I caught him on his way to work at the resort. I almost made him late, but he was patient and answered all my questions."

Pulling up the photo of the waiter, Hendrix asked, "Did that staff member have any resemblance to this guy?"

"No. This guy looked like he'd just turned eighteen. Way too young." Jax pulled the computer his way a fraction and clicked on a photo showing the staff member. There was something similar about him, but Jax was right. The waiter was at least ten years older than the hotel staff member.

Hendrix's shoulders sagged. "Okay. That's a bust too."

Ryder pulled up another video. "What got him was all the video footage, really. Then catching him cutting the wires. It's him." He stood. "Maybe you just don't want Britney feeling bad that she misjudged David. It does tend to rattle people and put a kink in their confidence."

"Yeah, maybe." Hendrix looked at Ryder. "I'm going to look through it again and then head back to the resort."

"I'm going to finish packing."

"Yeah, see you later." Hendrix returned his attention to the screen.

Jax dropped into the chair. "He has a point about Britney."

"Yeah, I know. Jax, I just can't shake this feeling, though."

"All right, let's play it again."

On the third pass, Hendrix slowed the frames down. By the end, he was so frustrated with himself. "Okay, I was wrong. That's all I can figure. My stupid hunch was off."

Jax tapped him on the arm. "Nah, you need to follow that instinct. It's better to be absolutely sure than have those types of niggling questions in the back of your mind, hounding you."

"I guess," he said and stood, pushing the chair under the table. "I'm going to head back to the resort. I'll see you later."

"Later."

Hendrix left the room and headed to the car. What a waste of time. He'd missed lunch with Britney and her mom, and for what? A stupid feeling. The worst part was that he still felt that way.

Britney had been upset when she found out it was David. Hendrix had hated the look in her eyes that she'd trusted the man and hadn't picked up on it. There was a really good chance Ryder was right and Britney's pain was the reason Hendrix was having so many doubts.

What he needed to do was move on. More than likely, some of the reason behind questioning David's guilt was that with the stalker apprehended, Hendrix didn't have a reason to pretend with Britney anymore. More than that, she didn't have a reason.

In his heart, he knew that wasn't true, but he'd lived with fear and doubt so long that it was hard to turn it off. He'd felt confident last night. About his feelings for her, and her feelings for him. One of the reasons he'd been keen on telling her about his past. He was almost a hundred percent sure that she'd care about him anyway.

The one percent remaining had a lot more power, though. Perhaps that was why the previous night had ended without him spilling all his secrets. Maybe the universe hadn't smiled down on him. At least, not in a long-term way. It was possible that the original arrangement of parting as friends was the best outcome.

His heart cringed at the thought, but there it was in all its ugly glory. She didn't have a need for him anymore. The case was over, and she could go back to her life. The life of fancy parties and dinners and men who ran in those circles Hendrix would never fit in.

He'd told her about his home life as a kid, but his situation wasn't unique. A lot of kids were subjected to that. It was the timeframe when Hendrix began making decisions that changed things. *He'd* run away from home. *He'd* joined a gang. *He'd* made a mess of his life by the time he was fourteen, and no one was to blame but him.

Britney was a sweet woman. She poured her heart into people, and it was a beautiful thing. But she was wholly unaware of how deep Hendrix's well was, and if he allowed her to invest in him, she wouldn't be the loving, vivacious woman he'd met nearly a week ago. He couldn't do that to her.

Plus, she was a billionaire. That life came with certain expectations—especially when it came to the people she surrounded herself with.

The first night they arrived in Oahu, she'd been frightened, and then she'd seen him attacked. In his line of work, that messed with people's heads. It shifted reality a little, forced people together. Made them feel things they otherwise wouldn't.

Hendrix appreciated her down-to-earth nature, but he needed to put his feet on solid ground again. Of course, that came with gently backing away, which he was sure would hurt her, but he'd agreed to be hers for the week. That was all he had and all he could give her. She'd realize in a few weeks that he was right. Now that she no longer had a stalker, she could go back to the type of men she'd dated in the past.

It was better for her, even if it broke his heart. If he loved her...

He stopped as he reached the car and braced his hands against the roof. He'd been so careful to keep those words from forming. Why now? Especially when he knew he couldn't stay with her?

Even if he told her all his secrets and she locked them away, there was no guarantee that they wouldn't come out later on. He'd killed someone, justified or not. All this time, he thought if he told her, things would be okay and he'd tell her how he felt. Fate had a way of stepping in when he least expected it. He'd held back because deep down he knew they would come to an end.

He could handle being crushed, and this way, she might be hurt for a little while, but she'd get over it and move on. To bigger and better things. A life she deserved with a man who didn't have blood on his hands.

21

As Britney stepped onto the party bus she'd rented for Ruby's bachelorette party, the driver greeted her with a nod. "Welcome aboard."

Again, the strange feeling of knowing him—like the other men—hit her. What was with her thinking that she recognized these random people? This guy seemed so familiar, but he looked nothing like the other two. Aside from the fact that the portly man looked to be nearly double their age—maybe more—he had a handlebar mustache.

"Thank you. We'll try to keep it from getting too wild." She grinned.

"No problem if it does. That's why we provide the transportation." He rolled one of the ends of his mustache. "Is the itinerary the same as the one you sent in?"

She slowly nodded. He sounded familiar too. How silly. David was caught. He was on film. This was just a carryover from looking over her shoulder so long. This poor man had nothing to do with it. "Yes, sir, it sure is."

"I'm old, but sir isn't necessary." His eyes creased as his lips quirked up. "Call me Terry."

"Thank you," she said and turned her attention to the six ladies seated on the bus. "Who's ready to party?"

Since Britney was the party-planning type, Ruby had given the bachelorette party to her instead of Faith. Actually, they'd both asked Britney to do it since they knew she had Harley to help her.

It had been so fun to put it together. Most of it was done before she even arrived on the island. She'd called months ago, setting things up so she wouldn't have to worry about it.

Her only problem was spending the evening without Hendrix. They'd been joined at the hip all week. It made his absence more noticeable. He'd skipped lunch to reexamine the evidence against David. It was so sweet, but Hendrix had acted strange during the rehearsal and dinner. He'd said he was fine, so she'd let it be. She'd attributed the attitude change to finding out he'd been wrong. Guys like him didn't like that. Being wrong was a good way to get someone hurt in their line of work.

The group cheered, and Ruby said, "I'm definitely ready. I can't believe it's my last night as Ruby Garcia."

Faith hugged her. "Me either."

Britney picked up the paper bag she'd brought with her and walked to Ruby, taking a seat next to her.

"Are you ladies ready to leave?" the driver asked.

"Oh, yes, thank you," Britney replied, and the bus began to move.

She angled herself toward Ruby. "Okay. We have a sash, a crown, and a couple of games to play tonight. At the end of the evening, the bus will be taking us on a relaxing ride around Oahu." She dug out the crown and set it on Ruby's head and reached back in for the sash, handing it to Faith to open so she could put it on Ruby.

"The bus is letting us off about a half-mile from the salon I rented. Once we get there, you'll be doing a ring hunt." She wiggled in her seat. "On the way there, you've got a photo challenge. Both games will have a winner, and they'll receive a gift certificate for a spa day."

Ruby grinned wide. "Oh, yay."

"We're getting our mani-pedis tonight. That way it won't be so hectic tomorrow."

"Aw, Britney, thank you," Ruby said. "I booked that already, though."

Britney gave a single shoulder shrug. "I know, and that's who's doing it. We conspired together."

"That sounds so much better than trying to get that and my makeup done tomorrow." Ruby hugged her. "You're always so sweet and thoughtful."

Faith leaned across Ruby and patted Britney's leg. "You are. Thank you so much for planning this. I would have, but I stink at them. I would never have thought of all this."

"You can thank Harley Wolf for that. She's the one who helped me brainstorm."

The bus came to a stop, and the driver twisted in his seat. "We're at the drop-off location."

"All right, ladies, let's get out there so y'all can take photos." Britney stood, motioning with her hands to move the women along. As she got to the front, she stopped at the door. "Thank you for the ride. We'll see you in a little while."

The man nodded. "It's my pleasure, sweet lady."

Why did that send chills down her spine? David had ruined her. Stupid stalking business. The driver was just being friendly. "Thank you."

She stepped off the bus and caught up with the other women. It was a perfect night for taking a stroll, and there was plenty of nightlife to make it easy to fill out their photo challenge cards. Faith ended up winning that one, but that didn't surprise anyone as she was the most competitive.

Britney hadn't just rented a salon. Each member of the party got their own tech. When she'd mentioned her idea to Harley, she was the one who gave her that gem of advice. It would have taken all night if she'd only hired one or two.

They hunted down the rings first, and one of the other bridesmaids won the prize. Faith wasn't particularly thrilled since she lost, but she was gracious about it since she'd already won a prize.

"Oh, I needed this," Ruby said. "To just sit a second. I feel like I've been running nonstop all week."

Faith chuckled. "You have."

"Weddings are stressful. I'm glad you get a moment to relax." Britney smiled. She needed it too, especially after last night.

Laying her head against the chair, her mind wandered as she listened to the women talk. Dresses, wedding cakes, flowers, music, and all the other things that came with getting married. Doug didn't mind giving all the control to Ruby. Oh, he participated some since there was cake testing.

Would Hendrix want to give her all the responsibility, or would he want to share it? That's what she would want. It would be more fun, that's for sure. Then she shook her head. She didn't need to get ahead of herself.

A knock came from the door, and one of the techs looked around. "Uh, are we expecting anyone?"

"One of the ladies left their phone on the bus. I'm just returning it."

"Oh, that's the bus driver," Ruby said, checking for her phone. "Got mine."

The other ladies went into a frenzy of looking for their phones, including Britney. She held her hand up. "I'm the lucky winner." And she was calf-deep in water, too.

"I'll get it." Her nail tech went to the door and opened it.

"Thank you, Terry," Britney called out as her phone was handed to her. She checked it, hoping Hendrix had maybe sent her a text. If she was feeling his absence, was he feeling hers? But there was nothing from him. A bit of a bummer, but it was just one night. They could both survive a night without the other.

"I think I know who's getting married after Faith," Ruby said in a sing-song tone. "Britney Wolf."

"What?" Britney came out of her thought fog.

"Getting married. I see how you and Hendrix look at each other. That's love, girl."

"Oh, posh," Britney said, working to keep her face

neutral. It was a losing battle, though, because heat flooded her cheeks. "We haven't been dating long enough for that." None of them knew how the relationship started or that she'd had a stalker for months. Now that it was over, she didn't feel the need to tell them either. This was about Ruby, and Britney didn't want to take away from that.

"Do you love him?" asked Faith.

"To the moon and back and twice again." Britney set her phone on the tray attached to her chair. "I have never felt like this before."

Ruby grinned. "That's how I feel about Doug."

Faith got a dreamy look on her face. "Same for me with James."

After that, the conversation took off in a range of directions. Guesses on who was next after Faith. Who would catch the bridal bouquet? If those old wives' tales actually came true. Fun and frivolity. Something Britney had needed without understanding exactly what she was missing.

With their manicures and pedicures, they returned to the bus and continued the conversation. Britney had the option of including champagne, but Ruby didn't drink alcohol. Which was fine with Britney since she could take it or leave it. No one complained either.

It was well after midnight when they returned to the

resort. Being the one who rented the bus, Britney straggled behind to thank him. "This was a lot of fun. My friend had a blast." She pulled out a bill from her clutch and handed it to him. "Thank you again."

As the man took the bill, his hand brushed against hers, and it took work not to recoil. Maybe Hendrix was right and having a stalker had bothered her a whole lot more than she realized.

"Thank you, Britney. It was a pleasure driving you around tonight."

"Have a good night," Britney said and caught up with Ruby and the rest of the bridesmaids.

It was time to set that whole ordeal to the side and stop letting her mind play tricks on her. That's all it was. Had to be. Again, she reminded herself that she'd seen the proof. She just needed to shake it off and go back to living her life. Although, she was thankful for Hendrix. Something great had come out of something terrible. For that, she'd be forever grateful.

22

Sitting beachside at Ruby's wedding, Hendrix kept his eyes on the water. Being the plus-one of a member of the bridal party, he was early, along with a few others. They were scattered around the two hundred chairs guests would be occupying soon. He'd staked a claim on the back row, closest to the beach.

He had so much on his mind. It had been a constant war since leaving Noah's hotel room the day before. He loved Britney. Something he'd never expected to feel for anyone. That had been his plan for almost as long as he'd been alive.

Britney had certainly upended that.

Now that he knew what it was like to be...cared

about, he balked at the thought of going back to solitary confinement. That was a lonely box to begin with, and now that it had a window, he was too tempted to sit in front of it and wish for something more.

"I've seen that look on a man's face before."

Hendrix slapped on a smile and faced April. "Boredom?"

Eyeing him, she made her way to the chair next to him and sat. "Battle fatigue."

"I'm all right."

"I see." She leaned back in the chair and crossed her feet at the ankles. Minutes ticked by, and the silence grew uncomfortable. "I'm sure you know that my husband passed away from an inoperable brain tumor."

"Yes, ma'am. Noah's told me a little. Britney too." Together, they'd painted a picture of a man who was kind most of his life.

"Being the youngest, Britney was subjected to his deteriorating behavior the longest. He was brutal, verbally, and the last few weeks of his life, he turned violent."

"I'm sorry to hear that. It must have been hard."

"It was," she said, her voice soft. "Especially the last few days before he fell into the coma. We knew something was coming because Britney came home one afternoon to find him in the house, destroying things. Paintings he'd loved, pictures of the kids, books...just trashing the house." April dropped her gaze to the sand. "I'd been out too. When I came home, he'd already left, but he'd beaten her. I found her on the floor in a heap, battered and bruised."

Hendrix felt like the wind was knocked from him. "I can't imagine..."

"That's not the story." She paused a minute. "Right after that, he fell into the coma, and my little girl, still black and blue, stayed with him the last week of his life. One evening, I was coming to sit with him so she could go home, shower, and rest a minute. I found her sitting on the edge of the bed, talking to him, just hours before he passed away." She took a deep breath and let it out slowly. "No one knows this, and I'd appreciate it if it stayed that way."

"Yes, ma'am, but you don't need to tell me."

"Yeah, I think I do. I think I've been holding on to it for just this moment." She smiled. "It'll help you understand my little girl better."

It wasn't her he needed to understand. They needed to understand he wasn't the one for her. "April..."

She turned to him, touching his arm. "She's in love with you. You need to hear this. What you do with it will be between you and her."

"Okay. I'm listening." It seemed easier than fighting with her right before a wedding.

April again drew in a long breath. "My sweet little girl was sitting on the edge of the bed with the man who'd given her two black eyes and broken ribs, telling him she loved him and that she forgave him. That he didn't need to worry about leaving because she knew what kind of man he was. She loved him with all her heart." April licked her lips.

Hendrix had no doubt that was true. He could see her doing something like that, but they knew why her dad was making his choices. It wasn't in his control.

"Now, you might be inclined to think that it wasn't that big of a deal. You need to understand that we'd dealt with his verbal abuse and attacks for a few years at that point. Even knowing it wasn't his fault, I was struggling to forgive him, but not her. Britney has the biggest, sweetest heart." April patted his hand. "Like I said, though, you take this and do with it what you want. Just know, if there is anyone who can love you, warts and all, it's her."

"Yes, ma'am, I understand. I'm not surprised. She is sweet and kind and genuine." And Hendrix was jagged edges, bad choices, and a long rap sheet. There had to be someone better than him for Britney. A person who could take that sort of abuse and still choose forgiveness deserved the best. That wasn't him.

April smiled. "She is. Thank you for listening."

"Thank you for telling me. I appreciate it."

"Sure." She bumped him with her shoulder. "And don't worry about my approval. Not that she would listen anyway, but I like you too. My son is a good man, and you wouldn't be here if he didn't consider you to be the same."

He chuckled and shook his head. "He is a good man and a good boss."

Their conversation shifted to lighter topics as more people began to fill the seats. It was wild to him, seeing that many people at a wedding. He didn't even know half that many and couldn't picture a quarter of them showing up to his... This island was turning his head into mush. He was backing away from the only woman he'd ever wanted or loved.

Just as he shoved the thought away, the bridal processional song came on..."Keeper of the Stars" by Tracy Bird. The man Hendrix had called Dad loved that singer, and that song in particular. Thanking the keeper of the stars for finding the woman he loved. The universe was giving Hendrix whiplash.

Faith passed by first, and then it was Britney. Man, she was shining like a star, twinkling as the midday sun's rays bounced off her. Her hair was pulled up, showing off those gorgeous shoulders as she floated by in a flowy light-blue dress. In his mind, the color drained from it and he was standing in front of a preacher, professing his undying love and loyalty. This had to stop. He could only take so much torture. The keeper of those stars needed to get their head on straight.

He silenced the war going on in his head and stood with the other guests when "Wedding March" started. Doug was a lucky fellow. Ruby was a woman in love, and she glowed like one.

A little more than a half-hour later, it was official as Ruby and Doug faced the crowd and grinned like fools. In a way, Hendrix was envious. They seemed so happy. Who didn't want happiness, though?

April and Hendrix stayed seated as most of the guests filed out, waiting for Britney. When she found them, she weaved through the people and stopped in the row in front of them.

"Hey. It was pretty, wasn't it?"

Her mom nodded. "It was. Ruby's mom and dad would have loved it."

"Yeah, they would have. I'm glad her uncle was able to walk her down the aisle." Whether she meant to or not, her gaze flicked in Hendrix's direction, and he didn't miss it.

He couldn't put off telling her that this thing between them needed to end. The longer he did, the crueler it felt.

"Hey, could we take a short walk?" he asked her.

She looked from him to her mom and back. "Well, we do have the reception. Ruby will expect me to be there."

"I know. I promise it won't take long." He would make sure they didn't go too far. The reception was taking place in one of the large banquet rooms in the main resort not far from where the wedding had taken place.

April cleared her throat. "You two go ahead. If anyone asks, I'll tell them you're on your way."

Britney beamed. "Okay. We'll be right there."

Hendrix slipped his hands into his pockets and tipped his head toward the beach. Her eyebrows knitted together as she looked from his hands to his face, but she didn't say anything.

They walked a good bit, until Hendrix was sure no one would overhear them. He stopped and faced the ocean. "I've been doing some thinking."

She crossed her arms over her chest. "Uh-huh."

"I promised you that I'd be yours for the week, and now that we've caught the stalker, I think it's a good time for us to be friends."

"We are friends."

"Only friends." He turned to her. "Britney, you are a billionaire with friends who are billionaires. I'm a guy with a juvenile record. You don't need my baggage gumming up your life. You have friends and expectations. You know I'm right."

Her eyes narrowed. "You chicken."

"Don't resort to that."

"To what? You are a chicken. I'm a billionaire, so you can't be with me? What kind of garbage is that? I don't care who or what expectations are assumed of me. I care about you." In a huff, she dropped her hands to her side. "Hendrix, I am in love with you. From the top of your boneheaded brain to your two left feet."

"You say that, but this situation was stressful. You need time to process it. In a few weeks, you'll see that I'm right."

A lone eyebrow twitched up. "I am not some fickle little socialite. I know exactly how I feel. I love how I feel when I'm with you. How safe I feel. We like a lot of the same things, and the things we don't, it's okay. A relationship is about respect and compromise." She took a step and poked the *I promise* tattoo. "When I make a promise, I mean it. I love you. I promise you that."

He hung his head. "I'm sure you mean that. Right now."

"Is that just me, or does it include you too?"

"I keep my promises or die trying." He lifted his gaze to hers. "I'm not trying to hurt you."

"No, you're not. You're trying not to hurt you." She took his face in her hands. "I can love you forever, but if you never believe it, it won't matter. I can't fix that for you or force you to take a risk. I can't make you love me, and I don't want to."

He pulled free. "That's what I'm saying, Britney. You see the world through rose-colored glasses. You don't understand."

She stepped back like he'd struck her. Her lips pinched together, and he'd never seen a woman with more fire in her eyes. "I am going to go to that reception and cool off before I lose my temper and say something I'll regret."

"That's what they all say."

Her mouth popped open big enough to toss a ping-pong ball in it. She clenched her fists. "Were they from Texas? Because you can bet your behind I'm coming back." Her Texas accent soaked the words, and if he had a middle name, he was sure she'd be using it. "Right now, I'm actually torn between knocking some sense into you or beating you to death. I'd prefer the former over the latter, which is why I need a minute. I love you,

you knucklehead," she ground out through clenched teeth, her eyes filling with tears.

She stormed off and then stopped a few feet away. "Knucklehead!" She shrieked it so loud, he was sure someone on the other side of the world was giving the person they were with a dirty look.

He rubbed his face with his hands and groaned. This was the first time someone had argued with him. The few women he'd dated had left, and that was that.

Maybe he was a knucklehead. Well, he knew he was, but even more so now. Despite all his stupidity, he found himself grinning like an idiot. Britney had fought back.

She was right. He was afraid. More afraid of getting hurt than doing the hurting. Knucklehead wasn't the right word, moron was.

His phone buzzed in his pocket, and he pulled it out. It was a text from Britney.

Meet me at the bungalow.

Okay... He quickly added, *I'm sorry. I am a knucklehead.*

Meet me at the bungalow. Now.

His head fell back. Whatever chewing out she'd give him, he deserved it. He was in love with her, and there was no protecting himself from getting hurt. The only thing he would be doing was ensuring that he *would* hurt...for a lifetime if he didn't have her.

I'll be there in a second.

He needed to make it right. Tell her he was sorry for being afraid, tell her about his past, and then tell her he loved her. She had to know about his past first, though. That was the only way he could handle it. All cards on the table. If she still loved him after that, he'd know for certain she meant it.

23

Britney was so mad she was vibrating. So much that she was certain her liver was in her throat. That idiot of a man thought he was just going to tell her it was over and she was going to slink away all teary-eyed?

It was clear he'd never dealt with a woman from Texas. They didn't put up with that sort of foolishness, especially when they knew what Britney did, that he loved her. A man didn't kiss a woman like he'd kissed her and not feel that way. He may have been too afraid to speak it, but his heart was screaming it through his lips.

That's why he'd pulled back. He thought he was going to push her away and that would be it. Not only was she a Texan, she was a Wolf. Once she had a second to cool off, she was finding him and they were hashing it out. She wasn't going to pressure him, but she also wasn't going to let him wimp out.

Other women had let him get away with it. What they didn't understand was that he wanted someone willing to fight for him. Someone unwilling to give up and give in. He needed someone to push through all his reasons, take him by the hand, and stand there until the water smoothed out again.

As she entered the reception area, her mom caught up with her. "Is everything okay?"

"My boyfriend is stupid."

Her mom cackled. "Well, that's a simple way to put things."

Britney rolled her eyes, laughing with her. "He's been hurt in the past. People just toss him aside like he doesn't matter. He thinks I'm going to wake up in a few weeks and be just like all those other people. I'm not. I love him. It's over for me. I'd sing, but I'm too boney and can't carry a tune."

Her mom hugged her. "I'm sure you'll figure it out. Noah wouldn't have hired him or let him come with you if Hendrix wasn't a good man."

"I know." She leaned back. "I want to cool off a second, and then I'll go find him."

"All right. Go do your bridesmaid duty."

They released each other, and Britney began winding through the crowd to the table, sticking her hand in the dress pocket for her phone. She huffed, grumbling when she couldn't find it or the keycard to the dressing room. She'd probably left it in the changing room. People were still somewhat standing around. If she hurried, she could grab it and get back with plenty of time to spare.

She passed her mom again, letting her know where she was going, and then broke into a trot. When she reached the room, she tried the door and found it locked. Just as she was about to give up, an employee passed her.

"Uh, I'm so sorry to bother you. I think I left my phone in that room. Is there any chance I could get you to open it?" She wrung her hands. "I lost my keycard, but I'm with the bridal party." She waved her hands down the front of the dress.

The woman smiled and pulled a ring of keys from her pocket. "Sure."

Britney sighed. "Thank you so much." She stepped inside the room and found her pile of belongings. As she searched through it, her phone dropped to the floor, and she picked it up. "How did people survive without cell phones?" She laughed as she walked out of the room.

"I haven't a clue, but I know I panic when I don't have mine." The woman chuckled and locked the room again.

They parted ways, and Britney checked her phone. A text from Hendrix popped up. "I'll be there in a second? Where in a second? The reception?" She smiled. Maybe she'd already knocked some sense into him.

I'll save you a seat, she quickly typed out and then slipped the phone into her pocket.

The tightness in her chest eased, and by the time she returned to the reception area, she was ready to give a toast and dance with the man she loved, even if he really did have two left feet.

When she reached her table, she searched the crowd for him. It didn't take that long to get there from the beach, but he could have taken a walk before coming to his senses. She'd give him a few more minutes and then go look for him.

Her patience held through the toasts by Ruby's uncle, Ruby, and Doug, and she squeezed out a little more, waiting until Faith was finished with hers before quietly slipping out. Britney didn't want to be rude to the best man, but it didn't make sense for Hendrix to text her and then not show up.

She hurried out of the reception area, not slowing

until she reached the bungalow. Hiking up her dress, she took the steps and barged through the door. The first thing she noticed was the alarm. It wasn't going off.

The second was Hendrix. In the middle of the room, he was tied to a chair and gagged. His chin was against his chest, and he was slumped forward. Scanning the room, she slowly approached him and untied the cloth covering his mouth.

"Hendrix?" She slid her fingers under his jaw and gently lifted his head. "Hendrix, can you hear me?" She ran her hand over his hair and stopped as she reached a warm, sticky spot. Blood covered the tips of her fingers.

A small grunt came from him. She wanted to untie him, but if she did, he was going to face-plant on the floor. Maybe she could loosen them a little. She lowered his chin to his chest, stepped behind him, and worked the rope a little to keep it from biting into his wrists.

She returned and lifted his head again. "Hendrix, wake up."

His eyes slowly fluttered open. "Get out of here." His voice was breathy.

"What?" She tilted her head, trying to process what he was saying. "What happened?"

"Britney, you need to step away from him."

She whirled around, and her heart dropped. "Who..."

"I don't want to hurt you." The man's hand shook as he held the gun. "I've tried being patient, but you just keep dating these guys who don't love you like I do."

Britney's heart sank to the floor. Noah had left the island. Her mom was at the reception. It was just Hendrix, an armed man, and her. What on earth was she going to do?

24

Hendrix's eyes flew open, and he lifted his head. A sharp pain poked him right between the eyes. Whatever he'd been hit with was giving him a nasty headache. He shook his head, and his vision cleared.

All he could remember was that he'd returned to the bungalow, expecting Britney to be waiting for him. He'd walked in, thinking nothing about the alarm being off, and checked her bedroom. The next thing he saw was stars followed by darkness.

His head cleared a little more, and he realized he was tied to a chair and a man stood in the doorway holding a weapon.

"Leave her alone!" Hendrix barked.

Britney slowly stepped in front of him.

"Please, just step away from him." The man motioned with the gun for her to move.

"Do what he says, Britney," Hendrix ground out. "My team will be here in just a few minutes. There's no way you're going to get away with this."

"Your team left earlier today," the man said. "Besides, I wouldn't hurt Britney. I love her. She loves me too. She just needs somewhere where we can be alone so she can realize it."

She kept her body between Hendrix and the man. "You seem very familiar. Do I know you?" She tilted her head. "Your eyes... You're the pizza guy and two waiters...and the bus driver from last night. Terry."

Hendrix needed her to step out of the way so he could see the guy and read the situation. "Step to the side, Britney."

She glanced over her shoulder. "I'm talking right now. Shush."

"I knew you'd see reason." The man sounded elated.

"So, what's your real name?" she asked. "Greg, Chris, Terry?"

"Rick...Rick Turnell. You get your Halloween costumes at my shop every year, and I did a magic show for Kelsie, one of your nieces."

"Oh, that's right. That was a little over a year ago, but I remember." She sighed. "How silly of me. Kelsie so loved it. You were excellent. You sawed me in half, and she thought it was hysterical." Britney was trying to hide it, but Hendrix could hear the wobble in her voice. Fear. "I've been in your shop many times, admiring those masks you sell."

Masks? The magic-shop guy? Hendrix strained to see around Britney. Rick looked to be a few years older than Hendrix. A little pudgy with thinning hair.

The guy brightened and lowered the gun a fraction. "Yes, you do remember. I knew it. I just knew it."

"How did you look so different each time?"

Good question. Hendrix was curious too.

"I'm the one who makes the masks," he said, dipping his hand into the front of his t-shirt and pulling a mask off his face that rivaled anything Hendrix had ever seen.

Not a few years older than Hendrix. Slowly, Rick peeled off the crow's feet from around his eyes, pulled fake yellowed teeth from his mouth, and pulled prosthetics from his ears. Each change took a few years off. The guy was the same age as Hendrix, maybe even younger. It was the eyes, though. He'd been all of them. Both waiters...and now that he was mask-free, Hendrix could see the resemblance to the staff member as well.

"Wow. You are incredibly talented. I had no idea. Chris had gaps in his teeth. Greg didn't. Terry looked to be in his sixties." Britney balled her hands in the sides of her dress. Nerves. Hendrix suspected she was giving her hands something to do so Rick didn't see them shaking. Smart woman.

Rick smiled and nodded. "Really? You think so?"

"Absolutely. I couldn't do anything like that." She smiled. "And you own that shop?"

"Yeah, I worked for the last guy who owned it. He died and left it to me."

"That was nice of him." Britney motioned to Hendrix. "Do we really have to keep him tied up?"

"Yes. He's no good for you." Rick lifted his gun again. "None of them are. None of them love you like I do. You were so sweet to take care of your friend Ruby."

"You know Ruby?" Britney asked. "I didn't—"

"No, I just...well, I kept watch over you." He took a step forward. "Made sure you were safe."

"How long have you been keeping me safe?"

Rick lowered his gaze to the floor. "Since a little after your niece's birthday party. You were so nice to me. Most people aren't." His gaze landed on Hendrix. "Guys like him. They think they can do whatever they want."

Britney shifted sideways. "He's not a bad man. We didn't know who was doing these things, and my brother just wanted to make sure I wasn't in danger. Hendrix was here to guard me."

"I saw him kissing you."

"Yes...I like him. I was lonely, but now that I know you're here, we can go wherever you want." Britney smiled. "I just need to pack a few things."

Hendrix worked the rope, trying to loosen it further. "No. No, Britney." If she did... Obsessed guys like Rick were unpredictable. If she made him angry, there was no telling what the guy would do to her. "You can't leave with him."

"Well, of course I can. He won't hurt me. He loves me."

Rick shot Hendrix a snide smile. "See, she knows I would never hurt her." The guy's lip curled up. "Unlike you."

"Will you let me go pack?" she asked.

"I've already packed for you. That's why I was in the bungalow." Rick used his arm to wipe his brow. "I saw the two of you fighting on the beach. That's when I knew I had to get you away. Take you from all of this. Give you the life you deserve."

Britney nodded. "Right. I agree."

"No!" Hendrix worked his hands harder, trying to break free. "No, you can't go with him."

"You'll see this is for the best." She turned a little more toward Hendrix. "I'll go with him, and everything will be fine." She walked closer to Rick. "He loves me."

"Britney, please. Please don't go with him." Hendrix

didn't typically beg, but he didn't know what else to do. He grunted as he tried to loosen the rope. "Please."

She turned to Rick. "Would you give me a second to talk to him? Let him down easy so he'll leave us alone? If you know me at all, you know I don't like to see anyone hurt."

Rick walked to her, draped his arm along her shoulders, and hugged her to him. "I don't know, sweetie. He doesn't seem the type to listen."

Turning into him, she set her hand on his chest and smiled. "He is a little hardheaded, but if you give me just a few minutes, I'm sure I can make him understand."

"All right," he said and kissed her on the forehead. "I'll let you try. Don't untie him, though."

"No, darling, I won't."

Rick stepped out onto the deck, keeping his eyes on Britney. "There. A little privacy."

Britney folded her hands in front of her and approached Hendrix. She bent down until she was eye level. "I have to go now. You understand, right?"

"If you go with him, he'll kill you."

Her eyes locked with his and turned glassy. "And if I don't, he'll kill you." Her bottom lip trembled. "I can't let that happen. I promised. Remember?" She took his face in her hands, pressed a soft kiss to his lips, and whispered, "I love you. Oh, how I love you."

"Please, Britney, don't," he pleaded.

How could he get her to listen? If she walked out that door, there was better than a good chance that he'd never see her alive again. All this time he'd held on to his past, using it as a way to reduce his risk of getting hurt. Now...she didn't know what she meant to him.

Britney rolled her lips in, discreetly wiped her eyes, and straightened. "Okay, darling. I think he understands now. He won't follow us." She turned.

"NO!" Hendrix growled. He fought harder against the ropes, rubbing his skin raw. "Britney, please. I love you."

She looked at him, a pained expression on her face.

He hung his head. "I do. I do. I love you." He brought his gaze back to hers. "I love you. I can't promise I won't be stupid again, but I promise to always love you. Just please don't go with him."

Rick walked back in. "I don't know. He doesn't sound like he understands."

Britney walked to him, putting her body between him and Hendrix. "He does. He's just upset at the moment. Once we're gone, he'll be fine. He'll realize we weren't meant to be together."

"You think so?" Rick directed the question to Britney while keeping his sights on Hendrix.

"Yes, I know he will. He's actually a very nice man.

He wants me to be happy." She looked down at her dress. "Did you pack everything?"

"No, I didn't have time." He motioned to Hendrix. "That guy interrupted me."

"Is there any way I could maybe change clothes? This isn't the most comfortable clothing." She held out the skirt of the dress.

"But you're so beautiful in it."

"Thank you. It's just not something you travel in."

He took her by the arm, and she flinched. "You're going to have to learn how to dress for me. I like this dress." The way Rick's fingers were digging into her skin, he was hurting her. He was already slipping. Hendrix had seen it a lot. Stalkers finally getting what they wanted and it wasn't the dream they'd pictured. "We should get going."

"Please. I'll bring it with me. I can change into it again when we get settled." She smiled.

Huffing, Rick pushed her toward the bedroom. "Okay, but do bring it. That way we won't have to buy a wedding dress. That one's pretty." He used the gun to wave her to her bedroom. "Go on. Just leave the door open. You can change in the bathroom."

"All right."

"Wait. Give me your phone. We don't need anyone tracking us," Rick said, holding out his hand.

For a second, Britney hesitated and then nodded before pulling out her phone and handing it to him. "Right."

"Okay, go ahead and change so we can get moving."

She disappeared into her bedroom, and a short moment later, the bathroom door shut.

Hendrix worked his jaw, trying to think of ways to stall them in the hopes that someone would see what was happening and call the police. Maybe her mom would sense something was wrong. Silently, he begged whoever in the universe was listening to step in, to do something. He'd never loved anyone before. She was it, and if he lost her, he would be lost.

"You're taking too long," Rick grumbled and banged on the wall. "You need to hurry up." The guy was agitated and becoming more so by the second. Unstable was the best description. He began to pace, muttering things to himself.

Britney finally appeared in the door with the dress draped over her arm. "Okay. I'm ready."

Rick strode to her and yanked the dress from her hand. "What's that?"

"It's a book. Why?"

"You were going to hit me, weren't you?" He lifted his hand like he was about to strike her. "I should have known."

She flinched back. "No, I was going to read it."

"Then why were you hiding it?" Rick grabbed her by the neck and put his face in hers. "You're a liar just like all the rest, but we'll fix that."

He shoved her back and lifted the gun, pointing it at Hendrix. "I'll take care of him. We'll find somewhere safe, and over time, you'll learn to love me."

Britney screamed and lunged in front of Hendrix as the gun went off. The next thing he knew, his ears were ringing, and the impact he'd braced for never came. She was on the floor and motionless.

Rick started toward Britney. "You killed her!"

A roar ripped from Hendrix's chest as he pulled one of his hands free. He grabbed the chair and swung it like a bat, catching the side of Rick's head, lifting him off his feet and dropping him to the floor.

Hendrix reached Britney and gently turned her over. He yanked his shirt off and pressed it against the wound in her lower left shoulder. By his estimation, the bullet had just missed her heart. "Britney?"

Her eyes slowly opened. "Are you okay?"

"I'm fine. Why did you do that? I've been shot before. I could have handled it."

"I couldn't."

Not a second later, Noah, Ryder, Rufus, and Jax were pouring in through the door with Noah taking in the scene and then barking out orders. Jax rushed over to Britney and Hendrix, his phone between his shoulder and his ear, speaking with a 9-1-1 operator.

Rufus sniffed Rick, growled, and then lay on top of him.

Noah shook his head. "Ryder hadn't disarmed the backup system."

"We were halfway to North Carolina, and I got a weird feeling. Noah had the pilot turn the plane around. We were checking into the hotel when the alarm went off. We got here as soon as we could." Ryder set his hands on his hips.

Hendrix hovered over Britney. "Just stay with me, okay? Help's on the way. You're going to be just fine."

After he'd been a complete idiot, she'd put his life over her own. She'd dived in front of him without even a hesitation. Just flung herself in harm's way for him.

He sure hoped she was ready for forever, but he'd been serious. He'd promised he'd love her forever. That was a promise he wasn't breaking for anything.

25

Again with the hospital? Britney groaned and licked her lips. Her mouth could have been a desert as dry as it was. She opened her eyes, and soft light illuminated the room. It felt late. She shifted in the bed and sucked in a sharp breath at the pain.

In the next second, Hendrix was beside her. "Hey."

"Hi," she croaked out.

"It sounds like you could use some water."

She nodded.

He grabbed a cup, filled it with water, and set a straw to her lips. Cold, oh, so cold it almost hurt.

She drained the glass and took a deep breath, grimacing with the movement. "That really hurts."

"Yeah, it's going to for a while. You shouldn't have—"

"Hush. You would have done it for me. I promised you that I wouldn't let anyone hurt you again. I meant it. You said you believed me."

He hung his head. "I know."

"You said you love me." She grinned.

His cheeks lifted as his lips quirked up, and then he looked at her. "Because I do. You were right. I was just too afraid to say it."

"But you didn't tell me about your past."

"It doesn't matter. I love you, and whether you love me still or cast me away, that won't change." He bent down and kissed her. "I love you. I love you. I love you."

Her heart monitor beeped like mad. "Stupid machine. Clearly, it's not a mystery that I love you."

"When you're feeling better, I'll tell you everything."

"Why don't you give the second installment now."

He grunted a laugh. "Okay. Long story short, my dad got my mom hooked on drugs. Things got worse. People were coming in and out of the house. I'd lock me and Walker in the closet to keep us safe. I was about nine then."

"That's just awful, but you were just a baby. That's not your fault."

"Joining a gang was. I was nearing ten when this kid

I knew introduced me to some of his friends. A gang. I hung out with them for a while. Eventually, I joined. To get in, you had to prove your loyalty. My test was beating up an old homeless man."

She couldn't imagine how hard that must have been. "Keep going."

"My brother started kindergarten that fall, and Dad beat him really bad one night. He went to school with bruises. A teacher saw it, and Protective Services got involved." He paused a second. "It was just after I turned eleven. By then, I had a rap sheet a mile long. The more trouble I got into, the higher up I got in the gang. They couldn't pin stuff on me because the guys would say I was with them. At the time, they were the only ones who seemed to have my back."

"I can see that," she said. "What happened with Walker?"

"We had distant family that was willing to take him in."

"Him? What about you?"

His gaze dropped to the bed. "I was trouble, angry, and wild. They didn't want me. I was sent to home after home. I'd run away each time."

Covering her hand with his, she shook her head. "That's just awful. You were a baby."

"Maybe, but the older I got, the better I understood."

"What about the gang?"

He took a deep breath. "I think you should get some rest."

She narrowed her eyes. "And I think you need to keep talking."

A chuckle poured from him. "You need to rest."

"And I will."

"All right. For the next few years, I ran with that gang. They had an old abandoned house. I'd stay there. I turned fourteen, and to celebrate, the leader decided to rob a bank with me as lookout and getaway driver. We were going to have a party." He gave a dry laugh. "Anyway, we planned this thing, and it was foolproof. We got to the bank, everything seemed to be going fine, and then the cops came storming in. I didn't even have time to warn them."

"Oh, wow."

"Yeah. They arrested me along with the guys who held up the bank, but they let me go pretty quickly after. They kept our leader and let the others go a day or so later. I don't know what happened, but the guys began to think I'd snitched on him. I was walking down the street one day, and before I knew it, I was in a firefight. The leader had put a hit on me, and I didn't know it at the time. By the end, I was shot, I'd killed someone, and there was a city full of guys just itching to take me out."

"Oh, Hendrix." Her heart broke for him. To be so young and think he didn't have any other choices? How awful.

"I ran. Got out of town as quickly as I could. I was hitchhiking, and my arm was hurting. I was in bad shape. Somehow, I ended up in a little town in Alabama. I was hiding in a barn, and the rancher called the sheriff, Eddie Grimes."

"After all that, you got arrested?"

"No. That man took me to the hospital, stayed there with me, and when the social worker showed up, they talked outside a minute. He came back in, gave me hard look, and said, 'Son, this is a limited-time offer. You can stay with me, but you'll follow my rules, you hear me?'" Hendrix smiled, a serene look on his face. "That man changed my life. It was hard for a while. It took time to learn that I was a kid and I needed to listen, but he stuck with me. That man was my dad."

Britney cupped Hendrix's cheek. "You loved him."

"Yeah. I'd told my mom I loved her, but that was before I realized it meant nothing to her. Other than you, he's the only person I've ever said that to and felt it had any meaning. Right before I turned eighteen, he had a heart attack. We got to talk one last time." He wiped his hand across his mouth.

"I was sitting there with him, and he gripped my

shirt and pulled me close. He said, 'Promise me something. Do it right now.' I told him, 'Sure, anything, Dad.' Tears formed in his eyes, and he said, 'You called me Dad.' I told him, 'It took me fourteen years to find a man worth calling Dad.' He said, 'You promise?' and I assured him I did."

Hendrix took a deep breath, catching Britney's gaze, and she could see tears in his eyes. "He took my face in his hands. Brushed one hand over my hair and said, 'You are my boy. Mine, you hear. You put all those dark things away. You got a place in this world, son. You go make a difference. Show these people they were wrong about you. You show 'em, you hear? You're a good boy. A good man. Don't forget that. And never forget...'" Hendrix's voice caught. "'Never forget I love you, boy. Never.'"

He swallowed hard. "A month later, I joined the Marines. That tattoo? It was for him. I've tried to be the man he thought I could be."

Britney pulled her blanket to her face and wiped her eyes. "That was a wonderful story."

"I killed someone. It's only because of Eddie that my records were sealed and I've been able to have the life I have. Without him—"

"You may have had a different life, but the choices you've made since then are yours. You were a baby, trying to survive. That gang was trying to kill you. You acted in self-defense." Britney tried to push up and whimpered.

Hendrix stilled her. "Hey, you've got to take it easy."

She took him by the collar and pulled him down. "Why did you think that would make a difference to me?"

"It wasn't you. It didn't matter if I told you or not, I loved you. I was afraid to say it because once I did, that was it. I let my past hold those words hostage when the outcome wouldn't have been any different. It would have killed me to lose you."

Covering her mouth with her hand, Britney yawned. "You aren't boring in the least, but I'm..."

"Shot and recovering."

"Lie down with me?"

Hendrix stretched out next to her, his head propped up in his hand. Using his free hand, he pushed her hair back. "I'm hopelessly, endlessly, madly in love with you." He leaned down, touched his lips to hers, and held them there a second.

"I knew that night of the luau. The way you kissed me. You weren't using those words, but you were saying them nonetheless." She ran her finger along his jaw. "I love you. You are the only one I want."

He touched his forehead to hers.

She was exhausted and happier than she'd ever been in her life. She didn't know who to thank, but whoever it was had her eternal gratitude for giving her Hendrix. He was hers, and she was his. Even with a gunshot wound, all was right in the world.

EPILOGUE

Six months later...

Britney slipped one arm through Julian's and the other through Zach's while Noah stood with the other groomsmen. The bridal march began to play, and the guests stood.

Her eyes locked with Hendrix's, gorgeous as ever, as she floated down the aisle and stopped. Zach laid her veil back, and Julian straightened it. They turned to Hendrix and took turns shaking his hand.

Noah left the groomsmen and joined her brothers. "This is our baby sister," Noah said.

"And we love her dearly." Zach elbowed her.

Julian nodded. "We're trusting you with her heart. If you break it, we'll break you."

"And Zoe and our wives will help us bury your body where you'll never be found." Noah grinned.

Zoe, Mia, Harley, and Summer raised their hands and wiggled their fingers. "Yeah, we will."

"We'll help too," Ruby and Faith said in unison.

The guests laughed, and Britney rolled her eyes. "Oh my goodness."

Her brothers kissed her cheeks. "We love you. We're proud of you, and if Dad were here, he'd say the same. We hope you have a wonderful, happy future with Hendrix," Julian said.

"I love you three pains in the rear." She grinned.

She took Hendrix's hand, and he helped her up the stairs. As she stood across from him, she marveled at how much her life had changed in the last six months.

Poor David had all the charges dropped. Once everything came out, it was something out of a movie. Rick hadn't planned on framing David, but once he realized Britney and David knew each other, he figured it was the best way to point the finger at someone else.

Rick had flown into Hawaii before Britney. He'd gotten hired at the resort, the bus company, and as a trail guide, and he was the staff member who'd supplied the evidence against David. The texts Britney had supposedly exchanged with David were done using a device that allowed Rick to send the messages and then erase them. He'd created a mask that looked eerily like David and had used it the night the security system wires were cut. When Rick attacked Hendrix, he used flat weights in his pockets to make himself feel heavier...like David. He also hired someone to hack David's credit cards.

It had been a wild confession, and they'd learned he was connected to a murder in Mississippi. The most recent information Britney had was that he was awaiting extradition to face charges there.

Hendrix had convinced her to have a few meetings with a counselor. Being stalked, witnessing Hendrix's attack, being held at gunpoint, and then getting shot were big things that needed to be talked about. He'd even gone with her a few times, which seemed to strengthen the bond they already had.

Three months ago, he'd asked her to marry him. She'd barely let him get the question out before saying *yes*. Now, here she was, looking at him, delighted to be pledging her life and love to him.

It was a simple wedding with a considerably smaller guest list than many of the weddings she'd attended. The pastor gave a few remarks and spoke to them of the significance of what their pledges of love would mean. When they reached their vows, the man turned to Hendrix. "You've written your own?"

"Yes, sir."

"You dirty dog. You said we weren't going to do that. Made me promise and everything."

The crowd burst out laughing.

Hendrix shrugged. "Yeah, I know, but I had something to say."

"All right."

He stepped closer and took her hands. "I spent my life thinking I was worthless. That the world wouldn't care if I stayed or went. Then, I met you. You are beautiful, intelligent, witty, kind, and sweet. I'd say you have a feisty streak, but we both know it's not a streak." He used his hands and motioned them over her. "It's all of you, but I think that's the most wonderful thing about you. You're loving and loyal. You're the force of nature I was looking for and didn't know it. I was a dead man walking, and you breathed life into me. I didn't have a reason to live, and now I want to live as long as possible." He smiled. "I promise to love you, honor you, and cherish you until my last breath. To care for you when you're sick. I will be your best friend, your fiercest supporter, and your knight in shining armor. I love you with all of my heart, now and forever."

Britney squeezed his hands and held his gaze, working to keep tears from falling. "I think I can say my own vows."

Nodding, the pastor waved his hand for her to speak.

"You were my missing piece. I promise to protect your rough edges, hold your heart with soft hands, and be your home. You are worth everything to me. I promise to kiss you as often as I can. To love you with all that's in me. I promise to take care of you, to hold you, and be your rock when everything around you feels like quicksand. I promise to spend my life showing you how much I love you. I love you with all my heart and soul."

He rubbed his thumbs over the back of her hands as he swallowed hard. If she had to guess, he was working just as hard as she was to hold back tears.

The pastor then had them exchange rings and pronounced them as Mr. and Mrs. Wells.

"You may kiss the bride."

Hendrix pulled her to him, dipped her, and then kissed her like the world wasn't watching.

When the cheers and whistles grew, he straightened her, wrapped his arms around her, and winked. "I love you, Mrs. Wells."

"I love you, Mr. Wells."

Her heart was full, and she was happier than she'd ever thought she could be. She'd found the man of her dreams, and he'd helped the rest of them come true. Together, they'd tackle life. Living, loving, and weathering storms as a team.

For a list of all books by Bree Livingston, please visit her website at www.breelivingston.com.

ABOUT THE AUTHOR

Bree Livingston lives in the West Texas Panhandle with her husband, children, and cats. She'd have a dog, but they took a vote and the cats won. Not in numbers, but attitude. They wouldn't even debate. They just leveled their little beady eyes at her and that was all it took for her to nix getting a dog. Her hobbies include...nothing because she writes all the time.

She loves carbs, but the love ends there. No, that's not true. The love usually winds up on her hips which is why she loves writing romance. The love in the pages of her books are sweet and clean, and they definitely don't add pounds when you step on the scale. Unless of course, you're actually holding a Kindle while you're weighing. Put the Kindle down and try again. Also, the cookie because that could be the problem too. She knows from experience.

Join her mailing list to be the first to find out publishing news, contests, and more by going to her website at https://www.breelivingston.com.

facebook.com/BreeLivingstonWrites
instagram.com/breelivwrites
bookbub.com/authors/bree-livingston
amazon.com/author/breelivingston

Made in the USA
Las Vegas, NV
05 January 2025

15898651R00163